飞鸟集

[印]泰戈尔 著

松风 译

生活·讀書·新知 三联书店

Simplified Chinese Copyright © 2022 by SDX Joint Publishing Company.
All Rights Reserved.
本作品中文简体版权由生活·读书·新知三联书店所有。
未经许可,不得翻印。

图书在版编目(CIP)数据

飞鸟集/(印)泰戈尔著;松风译.—北京:
生活·读书·新知三联书店,2022.1 (2024.8重印)
(三联精选)
ISBN 978-7-108-07233-7

Ⅰ.①飞… Ⅱ.①泰… ②松… Ⅲ.①诗集-印度-现代
Ⅳ.① I351.25

中国版本图书馆CIP数据核字(2021)第166732号

责任编辑	赵庆丰
装帧设计	鲁明静
责任校对	曹秋月
责任印制	李思佳
出版发行	生活·讀書·新知 三联书店
	(北京市东城区美术馆东街22号 100010)
网 址	www.sdxjpc.com
经 销	新华书店
印 刷	三河市天润建兴印务有限公司
版 次	2022年1月北京第1版
	2024年8月北京第3次印刷
开 本	850毫米×1168毫米 1/32 印张5
字 数	40千字 图12幅
印 数	6,001-8,000册
定 价	39.00元

(印装查询:01064002715;邮购查询:01084010542)

泰戈尔自画像

我的心潮拍打着世界的岸边,在那里含泪用三个字作为自己的签名:我爱你。

MY heart beats her waves at the shore of the world and writes upon it her signature in tears with the words, "I love thee".

泰戈尔的素描作品

她依依的愁容,夜雨般萦绕着我的梦。

HER wistful face haunts my dreams like the rain at night.

泰戈尔手绘风景画

云朵灌满河流的水杯,藏身于远山。

THE clouds fill the watercups of the river, hiding themselves in the distant hills.

《飞鸟集》初版封面
（附泰戈尔签名）

歌在天空感受到了无穷，图画的无穷在大地上，诗的无穷在天空和大地；因为它的词语既有行走的意义，又有翱翔乐音。

THE song feels the infinite in the air, the picture in the earth, the poem in the air and the earth; For its words have meaning that walks and music that soars.

常读常新的文学经典

"经典新读"总序

意大利作家卡尔维诺认为文学经典可资反复阅读,并且常读常新。这也是巴尔加斯·略萨等许多作家的共识,而且事实如此。丰富性使然,文学经典犹可温故而知新。

《易》云:"观乎天文以察时变,观乎人文以化成天下。"首先,文学作为人文精神的重要组成部分,既是世道人心的最深刻、最具体的表现,也是人类文明最坚韧、最稳定的基石。盖因文学是加法,一方面不随时代变迁而轻易湮没,另一方面又不断自我翻新。尤其是文学经典,它们无不为我们接近和了解古今世界提供鲜活的画面与情境,同时也率先成为不同时代、不同民族,乃至个人心性的褒奖对象。换言之,它们既是不同时代、不同民族情感和审美的艺术集成,也是大到国家民族、小至家庭个人的价值体认。因此,走进经典永远是了解此时此地、彼时彼地人心民心的最佳途径。这就是说,文学创作及其研究指向各民族变化着的活的灵魂,而其中的经典(及其经典化或非经典化过程)恰恰是这些变中有常的心灵镜像。亲近她,也即沾溉了从远古走来、向未来奔去的人类心流。

其次,文学经典有如"好雨知时节""润物细无声",又毋庸置疑是民族集体无意识和读者个人无意识的重要来源。她悠悠幽幽地潜入人们的心灵和脑海,进而左右人们下意识的价值判断和审美取向。举个例子,如果一见钟情主要基于外貌的吸引,那么不出五服,我们的先人应该不会喜欢金发碧眼。而现如今则不同。这显然是"西学东渐"以来我们的审美观,乃至价值判断的一次重大改观。

再次,文学经典是人类精神的本能需要和自然抒发。从歌之蹈之,到讲故事、听故事,文学经典无不浸润着人类精神生活之流。所谓"诗书传家",背诵歌谣、聆听故事是儿童的天性,而品诗鉴文是成人的义务。祖祖辈辈,我们也便有了《诗经》、楚辞、汉赋、唐诗、宋词、元曲、明清小说等。如是,从"昔我往矣,杨柳依依;今我来思,雨雪霏霏"到"落叶归根",文学经典成就和传承了乡情,并借此维系民族情感、民族认同、国家意识和社会伦理价值、审美取向。同样,文学是艺术化的生命哲学,其核心内容不仅有自觉,而且还有他觉。没有他觉,人就无法客观地了解自己。这也是我们拥抱外国文学,尤其是外国文学经典的理由。正所谓"美哉,犹有憾";精神与物质的矛盾又强化了文学的伟大与渺小、有用与无用或"无用之用"。但无论如何,文学可以自立逻辑,文学经典永远是民族气质的核心元素,而我们给社会、给来者什么样的文艺作品,也就等于给社会、给子孙输送什么样的价值观和审美情趣。

文学既然是各民族的认知、价值、情感、审美和语言等诸多因素的综合体现,那么其经典就应该是民族文化及民族向心力、凝聚力的重要纽带,并且是民族立于世界之林而不轻易被同化的鲜活基因。古今中外,文学终究是一时一地人心的艺术呈现,建立在无数个人基础之上,并潜移默化地表达与传递、塑造与擢升着各民族活的灵魂。这正是文学不可或缺、无可取代的永久价值、恒久魅力之所在。正因为如此,人工智能最难取代的也许就是文学经典。而文学没有一成不变的度量衡。大到国家意识形态,小到个人性情,都可能改变或者确定文学的经典性或非经典性。由是,文学经典的新读和重估不可避免。

一、时代有所偏侧。就近而言,随着启蒙思想家和浪漫派的理想被资本主义的现实所粉碎,19世纪的现实主义作家将矛头指向了资本。巴尔扎克堪称其中的佼佼者。恩格斯在评价巴尔扎克时,将现实主义定格在了典型环境中的典型性格。这个典型环境已经不是启蒙时代的封建法国,而是资产阶级登上历史舞台以后的"自由竞争"。这时,资本起到了决定性的作用。

二、随着现代主义的兴起,典型论乃至传统现实主义逐渐被西方形形色色的各种主义所淹没。在这些主义当中,自然主义首当其冲。我们暂且不必否定自然主义的历史功绩,也不必就自然主义与现实主义的某些亲缘关系多费周章,但有一点需要说明并相对确定,那便是现代艺术的多元化趋势,及至后现代无主流、无中心、无标准(我称之为"三无主义")的来临。于是,绝对的相对性取代了相对的绝对性。恰似巴尔扎克、托尔斯泰在我国的命运同样堪忧。

与之关联的,是其中的意识形态和艺术精神。第一点无须赘述,因为全球化本身就意味着国家意识的"淡化",尽管这个"淡化"是要加引号的。第二点,西方知识界讨论"消费文化"或"大众文化"久矣,而当今美国式消费主义正是基于"大众文化"或"文化工业"的一种创造,其所蕴含的资本逻辑和技术理性不言自明。好莱坞无疑是美国文化的最佳例证,而其中的国家意识显而易见。第三点指向两个完全不同的向度,一个是歌德在看到

《玉娇梨》等东方文学作品之后所率先呼唤的"世界文学"。尽管曾经应者寥寥，但近来却大有泛滥之势。这多少体现了资本主义制度在西方确立之后，文学何以率先伸出全球化或世界主义触角的原因。遗憾的是资本的性质不会改变。二是西方后现代主义指向二元论的解构以及虚拟文化的兴盛，最终为去中心的广场式狂欢提供了理论或学理基础。

由上可见，经典新读和重估势在必行，它是时代的需要，是国民教育的需要，是民族复兴、国家发展的需要。为此，我们携手生活·读书·新知三联书店，以当代学术研究为基础，精心选取中外文学经典，邀请重要学者和译者，进行重新注疏和翻译，既求富有时代感，也坚持以我为本、博采众长的经典定位。学者、译者们参考大量文献和前人的版本、译本，力图与21世纪的中文读者一起，对世界文学经典进行重估与新读，以期构建中心突出、兼容并包的同心圆式经典谱系。我称之为"三来主义"，即"不忘本来，吸收外来，面向未来"。

除此之外，我们还特邀了相关领域的专家学者，为每部作品撰写了导读，希望广大读者可以在经典阅读的基础上，进一步了解作品产生的土壤，知其然，并且知其所以然。愿意深入学习的读者，还可以依照"作者生平及创作年表"以及"进一步阅读书目"一类内容按图索骥。希望这种新编、新读方式，可以培植读者，尤其是青少年读者亲近文学经典，使之成为其永远的精神伴侣和心灵慰藉。

需要特别说明的是，"经典新读"主要由程巍、高兴、苏玲等同事策划、推进，并得到了诸多译者和注疏者，以及三联书店新老朋友的鼎力支持。在此谨表谢忱！

陈众议（中国社会科学院外国文学研究所所长）

目录
Contents

导　读　成长中的泰戈尔　戴潍娜　1
进一步阅读书目　21
作者生平及创作年表　25

飞鸟集　1

译后记　松　风　107

导 读
成长中的泰戈尔

戴潍娜

泰戈尔的诗行,一向高朋满座。

春和景明的诗句间,多的是不请自来的读者,落英缤纷的子弟,及络绎不绝的争议。这不可谓不殊胜。诗乃法器一种。勾起争议是魅力,在任何时代都能持续引发巨大争议,则是一种魔力。

百年来,世人用各种误会的方式爱着泰戈尔。这位有着圣人面相的潮流之子,他不属于在精致修辞和对句间表演特技的杂技大师,也绝非怀揣火药和新知的领袖斗士。意外的是,历史让他在一次次翻译和舶来中,扮演了比之更为鼓噪和深远的角色……

迎神与驱傩

多年以后,泰戈尔卧床不起,依然记得在中国度过的那次生日。[1]当晚的协和大礼堂名流云集、笑靥交映,如同一颗芬芳夜明珠,引逗着京城一等一的才俊佳人。这个乱世中的曼妙之夜专为他而来。俏艳的陆小曼亭立在礼堂门柱前,积极分发着剧目册页。四方宾客怀揣新月社请柬款款而入。坊间交耳相传,为了排演这出泰戈尔名剧《齐德拉》,新月社同人们疯魔了几周,从布景到服装、道具,种种开支用度惊人。正式开场前,主席胡适操着黑白电影对白式的老派英语,致辞欢迎这位从印度远道而来的文学巨子,他手一抬,代表知识界慷慨送出十九幅名画和一方古瓷贺寿。欢呼声未平,他又郑重不失诙谐地宣布,梁任公今日给泰翁新取一中文名,竺震旦。来自崇拜者们的鲜花礼物掌声几乎让泰戈尔应接不暇,他彬彬有礼地起身上台致谢并发表演讲。紧接着,丝绒大幕徐徐拉开,冠绝无二的林徽因,初登台便惊艳四座,被赞"服装特出心裁,奇美夺目"[2]。戏台一亮,大鼎、神座、朱红殿柱,光是这梁思成匠心打造的布景就叫人凝神屏息。平日里惯于辞章间唱念做打的文人雅士今儿一个个扮上,演王子的是哈佛归来的张歆海,演爱神的是天生的爱棍

---

[1] 参见侯传文,《寂园飞鸟:泰戈尔传》,河北人民出版社,1999年,第253页。
[2] 《竺震旦诞生与爱情名剧〈契玦腊〉》,《国际公报》,1924年第2卷第26期,第5页。

徐志摩,林徽因饰演公主齐德拉,林长民则演春神,"父女合演,空前美谈"[1];王孟瑜、袁昌英、蒋百里、丁燮林等一众知识界能人在剧中龙套跑得不亦乐乎。随之登上历史舞台的,是以新月社和《晨报副刊》为中心的一圈崭新的知识分子类型。是夜,全剧从头至尾英文出演,单是林徽因之音吐佳妙,徐志摩之滑稽神情,就够报业津津乐道上好几个版面。不足一个月,台上的这对年轻人陪同泰戈尔刚去法源寺赏过丁香,拍下了那张著名的合影,后世戏称"岁寒三友"[2]——林徽因若梅,徐志摩似竹,泰戈尔如松。

这一年,泰戈尔64岁。清明时节,他从上海登岸,近五十天时间,在中国地图上画了半个圈。上海、杭州、南京、济南、北京、太原、汉口,如一幅徐徐展开在春天里的长卷,现代科学大大侵吞了神秘的疆域,但这片古老而日新的土地仍让他心有戚戚。他因此称自己的中国之行,是"一种进香的人,来将中国的古文化行敬礼"[3]。国民革命运动方才兴起,

---

[1]《竺震旦诞生与爱情名剧〈契玦腊〉》,《国际公报》,1924年第2卷第26期,第9页。
[2] 参见费慰梅,《中国建筑之魂:一个外国学者眼中的梁思成林徽因夫妇》,成寒译,上海文艺出版社,2003年,第33页。
[3] 泰戈尔,《东方文明的危机》,《东方杂志》1924年第21卷第10号,第126页。

当激进革命派时刻提防着成为旧社会的陪葬品,他却同时被某种高深莫测的过去和辽阔的未来激荡召唤着。

文学,在和平年代带来的是战争的艺术,在乱世带来的则是和平的归属。自打来到中国,泰戈尔就没有半个空闲的日子。不到两个月,他发表了近40场公开演讲和沙龙谈话,大谈"复活东方文化"和中印友谊。用鲁迅的话说,他"几乎是印度唯一的被听到的文学声音"。同时期,中国也没有他那样世界级的文学巨星。既然诺奖得主泰戈尔曾代表失语已久的东方,在西方世界里发言,那么兵匪交迫时节,各方势力自然都渴望借助他的声音,为中国乱局独辟一条蹊径。彼时,新文化运动正受到以胡先骕、梅光迪、吴宓为首的学衡派,章士钊打头的甲寅派和辜鸿铭等玄学派的三面夹击。鏖战正酣时,泰戈尔被几方拉扯,绑上战车,成为治愈民族创伤的灵药、福音,抑或是骗术、迷毒。懊燠的政治气候中,"迎神与驱傩"[1]同台共舞,就连周作人也忍不住发牢骚,文化界对其"不免有点神经过敏了"[2]。

不论泰戈尔情愿与否,在这片土地上,他拥有一流的

---

[1] 王燕,《从"撒提"说开去——鲁迅的泰戈尔评价刍议》,《苏州科技学院学报(社会科学版)》,2011年第2期,第48页。
[2] 周作人,《"大人之危害"及其他》,《晨报副刊》第4版,1924年5月14日。

朋友和一流的敌人。

泰戈尔的父亲戴宾德纳特·泰戈尔及祖父德瓦尔伽纳特·泰戈尔都曾经造访中国。[1]他本人则在20世纪20年代和30年代两次访华，每一次都在中国知识界掀起飓风。和争议构成反差的是，他每一帧都风和日丽的文字，恰似飓风中心的风暴眼——那几乎是他周身唯一的安宁之所。挺他的人，有文学研究会和新月派等摩登知识分子，梁启超、蔡元培、徐志摩、郑振铎都推崇他；请他吃过饭的有北京临时政府的头面人物段祺瑞、地方军阀阎锡山；送他礼物的有梅兰芳、齐白石、刘海粟、宋庆龄；给他发公告的人是溥仪。讨厌他的是谁呢？鲁迅专门写过文章嘲讽他，郭沫若、瞿秋白、茅盾、林语堂对他多有不敬，陈独秀干脆骂其"未曾说过一句正经，只是和清帝、舒尔曼、安格联、法源寺的和尚、佛化女青年及梅兰芳这类人，周旋了一阵"[2]，讥讽他要再得一次诺贝尔和平奖[3]，甚至邀约胡

---

[1] 参见英德拉·纳特·乔杜里，《泰戈尔笔下的中国形象》，"东方文化视野中的鲁迅与泰戈尔——'鲁迅与泰戈尔：跨时空对话'笔谈"，《绍兴文理学院学报（哲学社会科学版）》2016年第5期，第23页。
[2] 陈独秀，《太戈尔是一个什么东西！》，《向导》第67期，1924年5月28日，署名实庵。
[3] 陈独秀，《巴尔达里尼与太戈尔》，《向导》第67期，1924年5月28日，署名独秀。

适，策划在《中国青年》开辟专版特号批评泰戈尔，被太极高手胡适闪躲过去。

不要忘了，陈独秀可是中国第一个翻译泰戈尔的人。早在1915年10月，他就翻译并发表了泰戈尔《吉檀迦利》中的《赞歌》，并在注释中赞其"诗文富于宗教哲学之理想"。而时光到了1924年，陈独秀劈头盖脸写下《太戈尔与东方文化》《诗人却不爱谈诗》《太戈尔与金钱主义》等系列讨伐文章，鞭挞泰戈尔的"奴隶的和平思想"使得"印度、马来人还过的是一手拭粪一手啖饭的生活"[1]。仅仅九年，二人思想便分道扬镳，冰炭不相容。

从最开始的追随者，到最激烈的反对派，陈独秀绝非孤案。就在泰戈尔访华的流量巅峰期，新文化运动骁将纷纷出招。《中国青年》开辟"泰戈尔特号"[2]，对这位戴印度小帽的年迈诗人集中开火。曾翻译过泰戈尔短篇小说《骷髅》，并在自留地《小说月报》上大肆鼓吹过他的沈雁冰（茅盾），此刻翻脸道："我们绝不欢迎高唱东方文

---

[1] 陈独秀，《太戈尔与东方文化》，《中国青年》第26期，1924年4月18日，第2页，署名实庵。
[2]《中国青年》1924年4月18日第27期"泰戈尔特号"中，有陈独秀的《太戈尔与东方文化》、瞿秋白的《过去的人——太戈尔》、沈泽民的《太戈尔与中国青年》、亦湘的《太戈尔来华后的中国青年》等文。

化的太戈尔。"[1]向来文辞夸张泛滥的郭沫若,一年前还沉湎于自惭形秽,称在贵族的泰戈尔面前,自己是"一个平庸的贱子"[2]。且不说其忆起自己日本留学时初读泰戈尔诗之情景,"面壁捧书而默诵,时而流着感谢的眼泪而暗记,一种恬净的悲调荡漾在我的身之内外。我享受着涅槃的快乐"[3]。他甚至在访谈中自诩:"最先对太戈尔接近的,在中国恐怕我是第一个。"[4]然而就在泰戈尔访华不久,郭沫若转而斥其为"有产阶级的护符,无产阶级的铁枷"[5]。

诚然,泰戈尔的诗让人很快爱上,又很快感到不满足。但究其根本,在革命的文学史中,诗反倒成了诗人最

---

[1] 沈雁冰于1920年翻译泰戈尔短篇小说《骷髅》,发表于《东方杂志》第17卷2期。1923年9月末,他与郑振铎选译了泰戈尔的诗集《歧路》,发表于《小说月报》第14卷第9号。1921年到1923年间,沈雁冰担任《小说月报》的主编,刊发了众多鼓吹泰戈尔的文章,其中1922年2月10日出版的《小说月报》第13卷第2号的"文学家研究"专号中就有郑振铎的《太戈尔传》《太戈尔的艺术观》,张闻天的《太戈尔对于印度和世界的使命》《太戈尔的妇女观》《太戈尔的"诗与哲学观"》等。然而1924年,沈雁冰转变态度,写作了《对于太戈尔的希望》《太戈尔与东方文化》等文(分别发表于《民国日报·觉悟》的1924年4月14日、5月16日)批判泰戈尔的思想,并表示:"我们绝不欢迎高唱东方文化的太戈尔。"
[2] 郭沫若,《太戈儿来华的我见》,《创造周报》第23号,1923年10月。
[3] 郭沫若,《太戈儿来华的我见》,《创造周报》第23号,1923年10月。
[4] 郭沫若、蒲风,《郭沫若诗作谈》,《现世界》创刊号,1936年8月16日。
[5] 郭沫若,《太戈尔来华的我见》,《民国日报·觉悟》,1924年4月14日。

不要紧的部分。左派人士对泰戈尔的讥讽，大多与诗学无关，夹带着各色主义间的党同伐异。萨义德在谈论知识分子的忠诚时，笼统提到两个名字，一个是古巴的马蒂（Jose Marti，1853—1895），另一个就是印度的泰戈尔，认为他们没有受到民族主义的爱国绑架。[1]泰戈尔呼吁重振孟加拉语，对西方"邪恶的馈赠"[2]保持警惕，一心期冀重返梵天和心灵应许之地，这些非暴力思想在激进左派眼中堪比毒物，是"有产有闲阶级的吗啡、椰子酒"[3]。国家正饱受蹂躏，内忧外患，抗战一触即发，此时大谈内心安宁，委实太过奢侈，然而殊不知泰戈尔在印度恰是因为拥抱西方文明而饱受委屈。在东方与西方之间、传统与现代之间、民族主义与世界主义之间，这位克己复礼的诗人始终坚持着两边不讨好，左右不逢源的中庸之道。

他"坚决地站在中间道路上，没有背叛他看到的艰难的真理……夸大其词和走极端是比较容易的"[4]。世人尽可

---

[1] 萨义德在评论泰戈尔和马蒂时写道："虽然他们一直都是民族主义者，但绝不因为民族而减低他们的批评。"参见爱德华·W.萨义德《知识分子论》，单德兴译，生活·读书·新知三联书店，2002年，第39页。
[2] 以赛亚·伯林，《罗宾德拉纳特·泰戈尔与民族意识》，潘荣荣、林茂译，《现实感：观念及其历史研究》，译林出版社，2011年，第303页。
[3] 郭沫若，《太戈尔来华的我见》，《民国日报·觉悟》，1924年4月14日。
[4] 以赛亚·伯林，《罗宾德拉纳特·泰戈尔与民族意识》，潘荣荣、林茂译，《现实感：观念及其历史研究》，译林出版社，2011年，第308页。

诟骂他过分革命理想，亦可掉过头来怪他太过顽固守旧。像一场醉翁之意不在酒的拔河比赛，牵拉双方都急于从他身上索取一些正面或反面教材。他的文学因而背负了太多审美以外的功利化营生，不可救药地跟政治缠绵在一起。

不幸，亦为万幸。泰戈尔所面对的是个人和时代、中西之间、古今之间、雅俗之间的永恒缠斗与多重误解。这一切矛盾，仿佛水被吮进海绵，统统汇入他广博的灵魂，有如一声温柔的巨雷，那是"人类记忆里的一次灵迹"[1]。

过时与重生

喇嘛说，灵迹不会发生第二回。

可谁成想，泰戈尔的诗是一出循环上演的奇迹——它在临摹和翻译中一次又一次发生。一个世纪以来，泰戈尔都是中印情感中的最大公约数。《飞鸟集》更是收获了数量惊人的批评与模仿。几年前，冯唐翻译了泰戈尔，再一次将他推上争议潮头，有人将之称为翻译界遭遇的一次"恐怖袭击"。此后，再翻译泰戈尔的诗，变成一件非常危险的事。

---

[1] 徐志摩，《论坛·泰戈尔》，《晨报副镌》第112号，1924年5月19日。

几乎是一种魔性。救亡图存的年代,泰戈尔被迫卷进救国话语、科学与玄学、传统与现代的论争旋涡;文学日渐边缘化的消费年代,他亦可无事生非闹出一场论战。

文学和人一样,有它的生老病死。《神曲》和《荷马史诗》活下来已成伟大的标本,《飞鸟集》却依然是聒噪鲜活的小生命。秘诀就在于,它在每个时代自我翻新。某个历史语境下一度无法超越的范本,伴随着世风迁徙和人类自我认知的推进,不断转世,不断被赋予新的意义。如同一颗顽强的原始种子在不同语言中自由地生长,《飞鸟集》被反复重译,且越译越新。坦白说,这得益于原文的不完美,但同时也彰显了其非凡的韧性和弹性。泰戈尔的中间道路,曾让他前后受敌;他的文字亦如印度的人口般繁茂,让真金经得住火炼——它经得起翻译折腾,付得起口舌代价。

作为我国最早介绍和翻译的泰戈尔诗集,《飞鸟集》最早出现在1921年的《新人》杂志上,当初的译名为《迷途的鸟》。[1] 此后流传最广的当属郑振铎的译本,他于1922年和1923年翻译出版了泰戈尔的《飞鸟集》和《新月集》,兼有剧本《春之循环》。1913年,泰戈尔获得了诺贝尔文

---

[1] 1921年1月《新人》杂志7、8期合刊上发表了署名王靖的译文,译名为《迷途的鸟》,共有171章。

学奖，跟他一道提名的还有一个东方人——北大留辫子的教授辜鸿铭。就在那一年，他开始进入中国。民国以来，泰戈尔的译者阵容强大，李金髪翻译了《吉檀迦利》《采果集》，王独清翻译了《新月集》，茅盾翻译了《歧路》，赵景深翻译了《采果集》，叶圣陶、沈泽民、刘大白、黄仲苏、徐培德等翻译了《园丁集》，瞿世英翻译了《春之循环》《齐德拉》，黄仲苏、高滋翻译了《牺牲》《马丽尼》，江绍原翻译了《邮局》，梁宗岱翻译了《隐士》，冰心翻译了泰老的《吉檀迦利》。一众名家不遗余力地在报刊上翻译、介绍和研究泰戈尔，参与人数之众，发表文章之多，刊载刊物之广，为五四以来所罕见。一时间满纸争说泰戈尔，成为20世纪20年代中国重要的文化现象。其中《飞鸟集》的译本最为富饶，特别是当代以来，已知译本超过15种，其中有郑振铎不断再版的经典译本，有传统文人姚华以古典诗词形式译出的《五言飞鸟集》，亦有冯唐这般的调侃和突袭。今年，我们又读到了松风纯粹华美的译本，将泰诗从庸俗化中拯救。花式百出的翻译，都得以在泰戈尔诗行中各自栖息，美美与共，这恐怕又是泰翁的一大魅力。

据说，让·科克托写于1903年的戏剧《人类的声音》是"全世界女演员最想演的剧本"。《飞鸟集》恐怕也是译者们最愿意去挑战的翻译。它给予了翻译者最大限度的自我。泰戈尔的译者,都像勇敢的演员,他们用自己的血肉、思想、文辞、个性重新将他在中文世界里演绎。如同一出所有演员争相冒头的戏剧——几个简单的道具、只言片词的短语、简洁的布景,这个舞台没有规定性,朴素的台词却变化万端,角色的性格全由译者定义。你尽可以在舞台上演出你自己,而这原本是翻译的大忌——泰戈尔又一次肇事,挑起翻译界的天问:究竟是读者优先,还是作者优先?译者弑君篡位,究竟该被历史接纳,抑或诛杀?支持冯唐的人抬出德国功能翻译学派的"目的论",反对者则搬出"信达雅"三座大山予以镇压。人们都说,老泰气得要掀棺材盖了!可谁晓得,墓床上静观的泰戈尔是不是在暗自等待另一位译者来证明冯唐还不够激进?

"一生中都是用一种美学的态度来对待哲学问题"[1]的泰戈尔,崇尚的是"梵",亦即万物有灵。基督教和印度教都是他的好老师。如果我们将他放在经学系统中加以考察,他的诗歌大门夜不闭户,清风徐徐般的性灵,乃是由梵音生发而来的对人的启迪。

一千个人就可以有一千种对经的读解。

---

[1] 维西瓦纳特·S.纳拉万,《泰戈尔评传》,刘文哲、何文安译,重庆出版社,1985年,第41页。

一个过客,不必装备任何时代背景知识,连艺术修养也非必需,就能眠进他的鸟语花香。他像诗歌界的莫扎特,听多了兴许会腻味,却真真切切敞开怀抱迎接各路毫无准备的聆听者。那是自德彪西以来,现代艺术丧失已久的纯真与可爱,是一番清澈见底的永恒。没有知识的疾病,没有艺术的疯癫,这些稚气的诗句,保持着早已被艺术抛弃的珍贵健康和天然和睦。如同1913年中文世界首篇引进泰戈尔的文章所言,"不在知世界之有苦痛,而在知转苦为乐、转忧为喜"[1]。

当卢梭、瓦格纳、波德莱尔竭尽全力从根本上改变人们对事物的感知,泰戈尔朝着后退的方向,努力让事物保持原样。他以少见的直觉,轻而易举地走入客体,走入事物的核心。如同一个打坐之人,拒绝艺术上的现代化革命,有意创造一种道德和灵性上的优越。他因而绝不承认自己食古不化。1924年泰戈尔在北京一度辩解:"物质世界的嘈杂极其古老。人类精神世界的揭示才是现代的。我立于后者,故我便是现代的。"[2] 不曾料想,他这番宜古宜今的

---

[1] 钱智修,《台莪尔氏之人生观》,《东方杂志》,1913年第10卷第4号。
[2] 转引自英德拉·纳特·乔杜里,《泰戈尔笔下的中国形象》,"东方文化视野中的鲁迅与泰戈尔——'鲁迅与泰戈尔:跨时空对话'笔谈",《绍兴文理学院学报(哲学社会科学版)》2016年第5期,第25页。

尝试，竟复活了中国自古有之的小诗传统。中国的新诗探索者们，多多少少都曾为泰戈尔所照耀。20世纪20年代，随着白话文的成长，传统文体都面临现代化转型。而不同文体，转变的难度大相径庭。小说适应语言环境相对容易（过去也有白话小说），散文次之，这其中诗歌的转型最难。中国古诗是严格参照格律，数着节拍写下的律诗绝句。白话文出现伊始，新诗的创作可谓一项创世纪伟业。诗人们几乎是在全然不知何为创作的懵懂中摸黑下笔。最初的新诗是胡适《尝试集》里那些潦草诗句，我们至今仍可以大逆不道地问一句：假如胡适错了呢？假如新诗从一开始方向就错了呢？新诗破壳而出，诗人们纷纷从各路语言中借来崭新的表达，刘大白、周作人、冰心等找到了另一种味道的新诗——深受泰戈尔诗灵滋养的小诗。

这些雏形中的现代诗颇有几分俳句的样子，实际上，泰戈尔的诗也脱不开俳句的影子，只是他不再恪守俳句那些严苛的规矩，比如必要的"季语"，比如五七五的铁律，又比如不能出现比喻——要知道，泰戈尔最擅联想比喻等形象思维，而非凯恩斯爵士的"用思想思想"，《飞鸟集》中比喻俯拾即是。俳句意象之间是直通的，是节制东方美的表达，泰戈尔无论如何都要更滥情一些，更有青春期特质。冰心受其影响写出的小诗《墙角的花》，至今还是中小学生修习诗歌的出发点。1924年冰心赴美留学,往后诗写得少了,小诗随之鲜见于文坛。泰戈尔的作品也日渐归为诗人们一去不返的青春期读物。

此等"过时"的诗句,大约会一直存活下去,只因人类也没有显著进步,只因一代与一代终究隔阂。

大道与小径

"一战"爆发后,泰戈尔放弃了英国国王授予的爵位,在美国亦遭冷遇。岂料"泰戈尔热"如一场热病,席卷了整个日本和中国。

这场热病持续了整整一个世纪,即便在不通文学的人当中,也引发了恣滥的迷拜与共情。令人惊奇的是,泰翁精湛的诗艺,并未灭顶于群氓之流,诗在诗人死后从未停止成长——它们持续成为人性中的一部分。《飞鸟集》一面过时,一面重生。

徐志摩在《太戈尔来华》[1]中提到:"问他爱念谁的英文诗,十余岁的小学生,就自信不疑的答说太戈尔。"这

---

[1] 徐志摩,《太戈尔来华》,《小说月报》第14卷9号,1923年,第1页。

位"最通达人情,最近人情的"[1]诗人,靠着"那种作为真正人类关系之基础的不可计算的人与人之间的爱与尊重"[2],获得了最广泛的信众。叶芝在写给萝西夫人的一封信里说:"现代诗人很多是将镜片贴近眼睛的金匠,但这不应该是你的道路,也不是我的道路,我们走在另一条大道上……那里有广阔的情感和传统的支撑,诗人可以大踏步走在人群前面……"现代诗羊肠小道走得太久,泰戈尔走向的则是另一个极端:他简直跟人群不分你我。网络上至今流传一首泰戈尔"代表作"《世界上最远的距离》:"世界上最遥远的距离/不是生与死的距离/而是我站在你身边/你却不知道我爱你。"查遍泰戈尔全数作品,也找不见这首诗的踪迹。这则心灵鸡汤最初出现在《读者》杂志[3],多年来"寄存"于泰戈尔名下,不断被报纸杂志转载,并收入语文阅读教材。然而,即便心知此诗系"高仿",还是挡不住出版商将其堂而皇之地印上泰戈尔诗集封面。一般而言,只有生平难以考据的古早作者身上才会发生此等错位。

---

[1] 徐志摩,《论坛·泰戈尔》,《晨报副镌》第112号,1924年5月19日。
[2] 以赛亚·伯林,《罗宾德拉纳特·泰戈尔与民族意识》,潘荣荣、林茂译,《现实感:观念及其历史研究》,译林出版社,2011年,第297页。
[3] 这首仿作为2003年第14期上的引诗,摘自同年第5期《女子文学》(现改名《女子文摘》),最初来源于网络。

一个现代作家,生平详尽可考,作品里竟混入了托名之作,实在是有趣的现象,也证明了泰戈尔非凡的吸收力——通俗的、高雅的、大众的、小众的、好的、烂的……人们坚信他都写得出来。似乎任何一首无名小诗都可以归到他名下。任何人都可以模仿他,即兴在车票、厕纸、烟盒背面写下几行生活感悟。这些即生即灭、随手丢弃的灵光乍现,十年以后没准儿就登上了泰戈尔诗集的封面。这种与"福尔摩斯""柯南系列"命运相似的同人自发创作[1],在诗歌界还绝无仅有。泰戈尔的文学世界从而有了一个开放式的结尾。

当工业化和消费主义瓦解了人类的共通连接,毁损了爱、忠诚和信仰的闭合电路,人类社会分化为原子化的个体和部落化的群体,泰戈尔用他人道主义的宽厚,在文学中重新连接起人类最基本的感性——那是属于梭罗和席勒所倡导的不含人本主义偏见的天真与朴素;是全然活在当下、毫无债务的精神满足;是内心深处从未开采过的灿烂;是人与万物之间纯洁的爱慕与尺度。仿佛春天就在他这一

---

[1] 同人写作往往发生于流行文化领域,在这种亚文化中,同人可以将喜爱的人物或故事抽离出原作,进行二度创作,也可将原作加以续写,改变情节,甚至混入原作之中。

方芳草地上复苏。轻轻一点,世间万象瞬间焕发出生命的光彩。

唯有季羡林窥探出其风光霁月中隐藏的怒目金刚。然而即便在最激烈的拉锯中,他泰然自若的文字也绝不带有文化讨债式的意气,泰戈尔从不和自己作对,也永远不会灰心。他所收获的纯熟的"金色的智慧"[1],夹带着印度的灵修文化和瑜伽文化,是古老东方不同于现代科学的另一套对世界的解释方法。东方哲学对生命的体认,找到了一个诗人的嗓音。"西方的人生目的是'活动',东方的人生目的是'实现'。"[2]当"向外求"的西方文明造成了骇人的浪费和精神世界的濒临枯竭,"向内求"的东方灵性试图治愈人心,开掘灵性的成长空间。

"人类之所以伟大是因为他的灵魂能容纳一切。"[3]洪熙注意到,泰翁的哲学同虚无哲学、周易哲学以及梁漱溟的

---

[1] "我攀登过高峰,在声名荒芜的峰巅找不到庇护所。引领我,我的向导,在日光褪尽之前,进入安谧山谷,在那里人生的收获将纯熟成金色的智慧。"参见泰戈尔《飞鸟集》,松风译,生活·读书·新知三联书店,2021年10月。
[2] 冯友兰,《与印度泰谷尔谈话(东西文明之比较观)》,《新潮》第3卷第1号,1921年10月1日,第139页。
[3] 泰戈尔,《在爱中彻悟》,《正确地认识人生》第五章,《泰戈尔全集》第19卷,刘安武等主编,刘竞良等译,河北教育出版社,2001年。

孔家哲学都有共同语言[1]，和王阳明亦有类似之处，既虚无又很有实操功效，商业社会的人群很是受用。某种意义上说，泰戈尔是现代心灵鸡汤的鼻祖。郭沫若则相信其泛神论思想，通向的是"我们中国同〔周〕秦之际和宋时代一部分学者"[2]。其"泛爱"与"疗愈"，远不只林语堂口中的"精神安慰法"，更接近于现代修行中的"身心灵"。不论《飞鸟集》还是《吉檀迦利》，都对上苍充满了奉献意识，是跟神对话的写作，充满规范自我的倾向与意识。"让他们活在他们自己选定的烟火啸啸世界。/ 我的心渴望您的星辰，我的上帝。"[3]

任世风百般变迁，任何时间任何地点泰戈尔都会是一位好教友，拥有亲和力的心灵导师，值得托付的可靠知己。难以说清，这究竟是一种前进抑或后退——在东方文明的根性中建造现代知觉，在现代世界返回梵天。然而不可否认，这套诗歌瑜伽，锻造出一派可供瞻仰的风采，舒展了一代代焦灼的心灵，熨平了无数公开或秘密的创口，医治了万千无法安宁的思想者。

---

[1] 洪熙，《太戈儿底迷途》，《觉悟》，第4卷第27期，1924年4月27日。
[2] 郭沫若，《太戈儿来华的我见》，《创造周报》第23号，1923年10月。
[3] 泰戈尔《飞鸟集》第286首，松风译，生活·读书·新知三联书店，2021年10月。

罡风狂浪中，泰戈尔始终是南亚的一盏明灯。没有他，印度和中国都要暗很多。

　　南亚次大陆的季风一年年灌进《飞鸟集》字里行间，这些"写于丝绢和扇子上的点滴思想"[1]，曾经乘兴而来，即兴赋诗题赠梅兰芳；也曾败兴而归，月老牵线失策徐志摩林徽因[2]；它们变色龙般，在不同时代换上适应环境的不同色彩，却永远能咬住时代核心地带的社会、道德和审美问题。结合了伟大和平庸，这些诗身段柔软，对付着善变的时局与人心，它们对这片霾天的造访还远未尽兴。

（中国社科院文学理论研究中心

中国社会科学院外文所）

---

[1] 泰戈尔曾说："《流萤集》，源于我的中国和日本之行。彼时我常常应人之请，将我的点滴思想题写于扇子和丝绢上。"
[2] 1924年泰戈尔访华，充当翻译的是徐志摩和林徽因，泰戈尔一度还想牵线，后来发现不成，当初还写了一首诗，即《流萤集》第66首：The blue of the sky longs for the earth's green, the wind between them sighs, "Alas"。参见泰戈尔《流萤集》（英汉对照），王钦刚译，四川文艺出版社，2019年，第66页。

进一步阅读书目[1]

泰戈尔著,郑振铎等译:《泰戈尔诗选》,人民文学出版社,2015年。

泰戈尔著,徐志摩等译:《泰戈尔对中国说》,译林出版社,2013年。

泰戈尔著,冯道如译:《远方的邀请:泰戈尔游记选》,江苏凤凰文艺出版社,2017年。

泰戈尔著,李鲜红等译:《和父亲一起去旅行》,江苏凤凰文艺出版社,2015年。

魏丽明等:《泰戈尔研究文集》《泰戈尔学术史研究》(外国文学学术史研究丛书,陈众议主编),译林出版社,2019年。

---

[1] 除书目外,还收录一篇诺贝尔奖官方推荐的印裔美籍学者、诺贝尔经济学奖得主阿玛蒂亚·森(Amartya Sen)阐述泰戈尔与印度的专题文章,以及联合国教科文组织《信使》杂志泰戈尔百年诞辰纪念专号,并附上两个官网相应链接。英文书籍中,不易获得的老书附上 Kindle 版信息。

Amartya Sen, "Tagore and his India" in *The New York Review of Books* (28 August 2001) ; Online version: Tagore and his India. NobelPrize.org. Nobel Media AB 2021. Tue. 20 Apr 2021. <https://www.nobelprize.org/prizes/literature/1913/tagore/article/>

Rabindranath Tagore: A Universal Voice, *The UNESCO Courier*, December 1961; Online version: https://unesdoc.unesco.org/ark:/48223/pf0000064331.

Krishna Dutta and Andrew Robinson, eds., *Rabindranath Tagore: An Anthology*. New York: St Martin's Press, 1997.

Fakrul Alam and Radha Chakravarty, eds., *The Essential Tagore*. Boston: Belknap Press (An Imprint of Harvard University Press), 2014.

Basanta Koomar Roy, *Rabindranath Tagore: The Man and His Poetry*. New York, 1915; Kindle edition, 2012.

Sarvepalli Radhakrishnan, *The Philosophy of Rabindranath Tagore*. London: Macmillan, 1918; Kindle edition, Paper Missile, 2018.

Krishna Dutta, *Rabindranath Tagore: The Myriad-Minded Man*. London: Bloomsbury, 1995.

Edward John Thompson, *Rabindranath Tagore, His Life and Work*. Franklin Classics, 2018.

Md. Anisur Rahman, *Social and Environmental Thinking of Rabindranath Tagore in the Light of Post-Tagorian World Development*. Dhaka: Bangla Academy, 2011.

作者生平及创作年表[1]

1861年　5月7日,出生于加尔各答市乔拉桑戈一个书香门第,是父母的第14个孩子。

1866年　5岁。开始随哥哥们学识字。

1868年　7岁。进入东方学校学习,后转入师范学校。写出第一首诗。

1871年　10岁。进入英印国际学校孟加拉学园求学。开始逃学。

---

[1] 编制本年表的过程中,深叹泰戈尔先生著述丰繁,人生宏博,这对每一个编写者都是极大挑战,笔者参阅的近三十份中外文献对诸多生平细节常常莫衷一是。每每想求助于一手材料,无奈不谙孟加拉语、梵语,只好出权宜之策,尽量选取权威之论,或遵从绝大多数,有时为厘清某一细节检阅当事人著述或英美学者若干文章。虽如此,错谬仍在所难免,诚望方家指正。主要参考材料有:"Rabindranath Tagore: A Biographical Chronology"(诺贝尔文学奖官网,转载自 *A Biographical Sketch of Tagore*〔Purba Banerjee, India Perspectives, V24, N2, 2010, pp.128-132〕), A Timeline of Tagore's Life and Work (Rabindra Tirtha), List of works by Rabindranath Tagore (WikiMili),《泰戈尔生平大事年表》(刘丹俊,价值网),《泰戈尔作品全集》(董友忱主编,人民出版社),其他恕不一一列出,在此一并致谢。

1873年　12岁。随父亲广泛游历印度,途中第一次造访父亲在十年前所购七亩荒地上建起的圣蒂尼克坦(Santinketan),其间写作第一个剧本《普里特维拉的失败》,惜手稿散佚。

1874年　13岁。完成《麦克白》诗体传译。第一次发表诗作,题为《欲望》并匿名发表。进入加尔各答圣泽维尔学校学习。

1875年　14岁。2月12日在第九届印度教年度大会上吟诵爱国诗篇《印度教的天赋》,并公开发表,这是泰戈尔第一次署名发表诗作。广泛参与文学活动,创作诗歌,发表叙事长诗《野花》。离开圣泽维尔学校。母亲病故。

1877年　16岁。1月1日在德里藩王宫颂扬印度女皇维多利亚女王庆典上,吟诵自创讽刺诗。创作第一个短篇小说《女乞丐》、长诗《诗人的故事》,在《巴拉蒂》发表第一部长篇小说《科鲁娜》(或译《慈悲》,未完成)部分章节。发表第一篇文学评论文章。

1878年　17岁。赴艾哈迈达巴德攻读英国文学,在《巴拉蒂》杂志发表有关英伦生活以及但丁、彼特拉克、歌德等文人圈里的浪漫爱情系列文章。9月20日第一次出国,赴英留学,在布莱顿一所学校就读。

1879年　18岁。进入伦敦大学学院攻读法律。其间常常造访大英博物馆，在《巴拉蒂》杂志连载赞美英国社会和人民的《英伦书札》。开始创作第一部诗剧《破碎的心》，写作长诗《覆舟》。

1880年　19岁。学业未竟提前回到印度，开始创作第一批具有个性基调的诗歌。诗集《暮歌集》问世，多数学者认为这是泰戈尔公开出版的第一部书。

1881年　20岁。第一部音乐剧《瓦尔米基的天才》上演，并饰演剧中的一个小角色。发表第一个公众讲演《音乐与情感》。《破碎的心》出版。4月20日，再度赴英求学，但中途从马德拉斯返回。着手创作第一部恢宏的长篇小说《王后市场》。

1882年　21岁。《晨歌集》问世。

1883年　22岁。与穆里纳莉妮·德维结婚。开始创作《画与歌》。

1884年　23岁。诗剧《大自然的报复》问世，翻译雪莱、伊丽莎白·勃朗宁、雨果等人的作品。兄嫂迦登帕莉·德维之死，令泰戈尔第一次体验到失去亲人的悲痛。被任命为"梵社"秘书。

1885年　24岁。接管孟加拉杂志《巴拉克》，为其撰写若干诗歌、论文、幽默小品、杂文等。联合编选毗湿奴抒情诗选。

1886年　25岁。为印度国民大会党第二次大会创作并演唱会歌。第一个孩子，即长女出生。诗集《刚与柔》出版。

1887年 26岁。着手创作《心声集》组诗,无论主题还是诗艺都显示出独特的原创性和活力。以笔名发表一位老派爷爷与观念现代的孙子之间的来往书信《爷孙书简》。

1888年 27岁。出版第一部文学评论集《评论集》。长子出生。

1889年 28岁。创作第一部五幕剧《国王和王后》,并在一次演出中扮演国王。创作名剧《牺牲》,次年上演。

1890年 29岁。严厉抨击克罗斯勋爵反印度政策。接管祖业。组诗《心声集》出版。努力阅读《浮士德》原文。游历意大利、法国和英国,旅行日记次年出版。

1891年 30岁。与侄子创办孟加拉文杂志《实践》,并撰稿。第二个女儿出生。

1892年 31岁。频繁游历孟加拉北部。撰写第一篇批评英国教育制度的文章《异想天开谈教育》,力主推行母语教育。断断续续习画。短篇小说《弃绝》《喀布尔人》发表。

1893年 32岁。开始写作由一系列关于人生、文学与艺术的精彩对话组成的《五行日记》。

1894年 33岁。为唤起公众对民间文学的重视,亲自搜集整理民谣、儿歌。当选孟加拉文学学会副主席,出任《实践》杂志主编。小女儿莱努卡出生。风格一新的诗集《金舟集》出版。

1895年 34岁。创作《饥饿的石头》等出色短篇小说。发表诗剧

《齐德拉》，后于1936年改编成舞剧。宣读论孟加拉文学前途的论文。《实践》停刊。创办国营商店，在孟加拉青年中推广本土货物。

1896年 35岁。写作《江河集》，合编《梵语入门》。为印度国民大会党第十二次代表大会创作歌曲并演唱。创作抒情诗剧《玛利妮》。幼子出生。

1897年 36岁。创作喜剧《拜贡特的手稿》，在舞台演出时扮演角色。

1898年 37岁。出任《巴拉蒂》主编，并撰稿。英国反煽动法案通过，泰戈尔在加尔各答公众集会上朗诵论文《被掐住脖子的人》，猛烈抨击英国政府反动政策。开设家庭学堂教育子女，延聘英国人劳伦斯教授英文，请印度学者教授梵文，自己亲授孟加拉文。

1899年 38岁。撰写全面梳理印度当代艺术发展状况的文章，引起较大反响。辞去《巴拉蒂》主编职务。着手创作第一部重要的长篇小说《眼中沙》，《微思集》出版。

1900年 39岁。出版诗集《故事诗集》《瞬息集》和《幻想集》。

1901年 40岁。任《孟加拉观察》杂志主编，直至1906年。在该杂志上连载长篇小说《眼中沙》，1902年出版单行本。经父亲许可，在圣蒂尼克坦按印度古代森林学堂模式创办学校，12月22日梵行院正式开学。

1902年　41岁。11月23日，妻子病逝，写哀悼诗，1903年结集出版，题为《怀念集》。创作长篇小说《沉船》，1903年在《孟加拉观察》连载，1906年出版单行本。

1903年　42岁。小女儿莱努卡病死。出版诗集《儿童集》。开始严肃思考国家面临的政治问题。

1904年　43岁。完成产生重大影响的《我们的国家，我们的社会》一文的写作。

1905年　44岁。1月15日，88岁高龄的父亲在加尔各答逝世。创办政治性月刊《宝库》。参加反对英国殖民当局分裂印度的独立运动。倡导建设性不合作对抗英国统治。

1906年　45岁。送长子罗提德拉纳特去美国学农业科学。发表诗集《渡口集》。

1907年　46岁。与领导民族自治运动的国大党领袖发生意见分歧，从独立运动中脱身，回圣蒂尼克坦从事文学创作和教育活动。出版文学论集《文学》。幼子去世。

1908年　47岁。主持孟加拉邦政治协商会议，用孟加拉语发表演讲，打破用英语演讲惯例。出版诗剧《秋天的节日》和散文剧《王冠》。发表论文集《国王臣民》《集体》《社会》《教育》和《自治》。

1909年　48岁。出版宗教、哲学演讲集《圣蒂尼克坦》1—8卷以及9—11卷。长子罗提德拉纳特离美回国。

1910年　49岁。孟加拉语诗集《吉檀迦利》出版。长篇小说《戈拉》出版。在《侨民》连载《回忆录》，1912年出单行本。写出剧本《邮局》，1912年发表。演讲集《圣蒂尼克坦》12—13卷出版。

1911年　50岁。创作歌词《人民的意志》，在第二十六届印度国民大会上演唱，印度独立后被定为国歌。

1912年　51岁。5月27日，动身去英国旅行，结识英国画家威廉·罗森斯坦，在其周旋下，《吉檀迦利》英文版由伦敦印度学会出版。6月27日，大诗人叶芝应罗森斯坦之邀，在其寓所与泰戈尔见面，此后叶芝开始与泰戈尔合作翻译《吉檀迦利》并作序。其间赴欧陆访问，结识通晓孟加拉文的瑞典东方学家、诺贝尔文学奖评委泰格内尔，此人对泰戈尔获诺奖起了关键作用。第一次访问美国，次年9月4日返回印度。

1913年　52岁。英文诗集《园丁集》《新月集》由伦敦麦克米伦公司出版。因"敏感深邃、清新美丽的诗，借助这些诗，以高超技艺使得自己的英语词汇所表达的饱含诗意的思想成了西方文学的组成部分"而荣获诺贝尔文学奖，成为欧洲以外第一位获此殊荣的作家。加尔各答大学授予诗人博士学位。

1914年　53岁。发表短篇小说《一个女人的信》。

1915年　54岁。甘地访问圣蒂尼克坦，泰戈尔会见甘地。7月3日，英国国王授予诗人爵位。演讲集《圣蒂尼克坦》第14卷出版，次年出版第15—17卷。

1916年　55岁。5月开始取道中国和日本赴美国访问，就民族主义发表系列演说。在美国发表题为"人格"的讲演。长篇小说《家与世界》和《四个人》出版。诗信《鸿雁集》发表。英文诗集《采果集》《飞鸟集》发表。剧本《春之循环》和短篇小说集《小说七篇》出版。

1917年　56岁。3月回国。在加尔各答的印度国大党会议上朗读诗篇《印度的祈求》。

1918年　57岁。国际大学奠基。长女去世。诗集《逃遁集》出版。收录《邮政局长》等14个短篇的小说集出版。

1919年　58岁。5月29日，写信给印度总督，抗议英国殖民当局在阿姆利则的暴行，宣布放弃英国授予的爵位。发表游记《日本记游》。

1920年　59岁。为国际大学募集资金，5月离开印度赴英国讲学，此行游历法国、荷兰和美国。旅美期间，与师从杜威求学的中国哲学家冯友兰探讨中西文化，后者将谈话录整理成文，题为《与印度太谷尔谈话》。出版短篇小说集《第二个》。

1921年　60岁。1月2日在纽约发表《东方与西方的交汇》演讲，

4日到海伦·凯勒寓所拜访，获赠《我所生活的世界》。3月从美国回伦敦，后赴法国、瑞士、德国、瑞典、奥地利、捷克斯洛伐克等国访问。在巴黎与罗曼·罗兰见面，在德国与托马斯·曼见面。7月回到印度。12月23日，国际大学正式成立，将圣蒂尼克坦的全部财产捐献给国际大学。《沉船》英译本出版。英文版《游思集》出版。

1922年　61岁。2月6日，与威廉·皮尔森等参与组建乡村重建学院。2月在国际大学主持纪念莫里哀诞辰三百周年活动。7月担任加尔各答举行的纪念雪莱逝世一百周年大会的主席。9月开始到西印度和南印度旅行。又到北印度和西印度旅行和演讲。12月长兄去世。发表散文诗集《随想集》。出版儿童诗集《儿童湿婆集》。发表象征剧《摩克多塔拉》。

1923年　62岁。将自己已发表的孟加拉语著作的版权献给国际大学。英文版《戈拉》出版。发表音乐剧《春天》。

1924年　63岁。4月至5月，应梁启超等人邀请，访问中国，游历上海、杭州、南京、济南、北京等地，并进行了三四十场演讲，引起强烈反响甚至争议。时任北京大学教授的中国诗人徐志摩担任主要陪同人兼翻译。在华演讲次年以"在中国的谈话"为题出版。梁启超在欢迎辞中，借机阐述印度与中国文化之亲属关系。徐志摩的送别辞情真意切，对争议做出巧妙而有力的回应。6月至7月，访问日本。7月下旬回印度。9月，应邀去秘鲁访问。因病在布宜诺斯艾利斯停留，其间创作的诗次年收入《黄昏之歌》出版。

1925年　64岁。1月4日离开布宜诺斯艾利斯去意大利热那亚、米兰和威尼斯。2月从威尼斯回印度。5月在圣蒂尼克坦会见甘地，但就不合作等问题存在分歧，拒绝甘地要其加入政治运动的邀请。年底，被选为印度哲学大会主席。

1926年　65岁。5月开始，受人误导以墨索里尼客人身份出访意大利，墨索里尼告诉泰戈尔："我是您的意大利钦慕者，您的每一部译成意大利语的作品我都一一拜读过。"此行还访问了英国、瑞士、挪威、瑞典、丹麦、德国、捷克斯洛伐克、奥地利、匈牙利、南斯拉夫、保加利亚、希腊和埃及等国，在瑞士与罗曼·罗兰见面，在德国与爱因斯坦会面。12月回印度。发表《红夹竹桃》《单身汉俱乐部》和《势均力敌》等剧本。

1927年　66岁。剧本《舞女的祭拜》在加尔各答搬上舞台，泰戈尔出演僧人。创作长篇小说《纠缠》，1929年出版。在巴拉特普尔主持印地文学会议，与青年作家论战。7月出发去新加坡、马来亚、印度尼西亚和泰国访问，12月返回印度。发表诗集《随感录》。

1928年　67岁。访问锡兰（今斯里兰卡），开始作画。创作长篇小说《最后一首诗》，次年出版。

1929年　68岁。3—7月，出访加拿大、日本和越南。发表诗集书信集《旅行者》。

1930年　69岁。3月开始第十一次出国访问。在牛津大学做希伯特系列讲座（出版时书名为《人的宗教》）。在法国首次举办个人画展，继而在英国、德国、瑞士、美国等国办个展。在《侨民》杂志上开始发表《俄罗斯书简》，1931年结集出版。

1931年　70岁。1月回印度。印度隆重庆祝诗人七十大寿。出版诗集《森林之声集》。

1932年　71岁。写诗文抗议英国殖民当局逮捕甘地。唯一的孙子尼丁德拉纳特去世。出版诗集《再次集》，剧本《时间的流逝》发表。访问伊朗和伊拉克。

1933年　72岁。在安得拉大学以"人"为题发表演讲。中篇小说《两姐妹》发表。诗集《五彩集》发表。剧本《纸牌国》发表。

1934年　73岁。率领国际大学业余舞剧团到锡兰和南印度巡回演出。

1935年　74岁。英文论文集《东方和西方》出版。《泰戈尔歌曲二十六首》出版。漫游印度北方，并在一些大学发表演说，为国际大学募集资金。发表诗集《小径集》。

1936年　75岁。在加尔各答做教育问题三演讲，英文论文集《使教育符合国情》出版。诗集《叶盘集》出版，游记《日本与波斯之行》出版，论文集《韵律》和《文学的道路》出版。

1937年　76岁。在加尔各答大学的开学典礼上用孟加拉语发表演说。在圣蒂尼克坦主持国际大学中国学院成立典礼。著文《印度和中国》。在加尔各答群众集会上发表演说，抗议虐待安达曼岛上囚禁的政治犯。9月10日突然不省人事，昏迷达48小时。诗集《错位集》《儿歌之画集》出版。短篇小说集《他》出版。

1938年　77岁。写信给日本诗人野口米次郎，谴责日本帝国主义侵略中国的罪恶行径。诗集《边沿集》和《晚灯祭集》出版。

1939年　78岁。诗集《戏谑集》《天灯集》出版。发表舞剧《解脱之路》和《夏玛》。12月，应泰戈尔邀请，中国艺术家徐悲鸿赴印度国际大学举办画展，并学术交流一年。

1940年　79岁。2月，泰戈尔在圣蒂尼克坦最后一次会见甘地。8月，牛津大学授予泰戈尔博士学位。9月，病情加重，被送到加尔各答就医。英文自传《我的童年》出版。诗集《新生集》《唢呐集》《病榻集》出版。短篇小说集《三个同伴》出版。徐悲鸿为泰戈尔造像，《泰戈尔像》融会中西艺术风格，成为传世经典。

1941年 80岁。4月14日，最后一次发表公开演讲，题为"文明的危机"。6月，口述最后一个短篇小说《穆斯林的故事》。临终前一直在思考生与死，口授若干诗篇，如《第一天的太阳》《黑暗的伤心之夜》等；7月30日9时30分口授了最后一篇诗作《通往创造的途中》，表明诗人已然拨散虚妄迷雾，参透生死，"拥抱了真／以它的光涤净了最内在的生命"。8月7日在加尔各答祖居去世。

飞鸟集

Stray Birds

根据泰戈尔译自孟加拉语的英文版
(纽约:麦克米伦公司,1916)译出

献给

横滨的T. HARA

1

STRAY birds of summer come to my window to sing and fly away.

And yellow leaves of autumn, which have no songs, flutter and fall there with a sigh.

夏天迷途的鸟儿来到我的窗前,歌唱,又飞走。

秋天的黄叶,无歌可唱,扑棱棱落在地,一声叹息。

2

O TROUPE of little vagrants of the world, leave your footprints in my words.

噢,你们这班浪迹天下的小小漂泊者啊,将你们的足印留在我的词语里。

3

THE world puts off its mask of vastness to its lover.
It becomes small as one song, as one kiss of the eternal.

世界对它的情人脱去浩瀚的面纱。

它变得小如一首歌,似永恒的一个吻。

4

IT is the tears of the earth that keep her smiles in bloom.

是大地的泪水让她的笑容绽放。

5

THE mighty desert is burning for the love of a blade of grass who shakes her head and laughs and flies away.

广袤的沙漠渴望一片草叶的爱,草叶摇摇头,笑着飞走了。

6

IF you shed tears when you miss the sun, you also miss the stars.

倘若看不见太阳时你落泪,你也看不见星星。

7

THE sands in your way beg for your song and your movement, dancing water. Will you carry the burden of their lameness?

舞蹈的流水啊,沿途的泥沙乞求你的歌、你的流动。你是否愿意背负它们这些累赘?

8

HER wistful face haunts my dreams like the rain at night.

她依依的愁容,夜雨般萦绕着我的梦。

9

ONCE we dreamt that we were strangers.
We wake up to find that we were dear to each other.

曾经梦见我们形同陌路。
醒来我们发觉彼此亲密。

10

SORROW is hushed into peace in my heart like the evening among the silent trees.

悲伤在我心里平息而安宁,恰似黄昏在寂静的林间无声。

11

SOME unseen fingers, like idle breeze, are playing upon my heart the music of the ripples.

某些不被觉察的指尖,仿佛闲散的轻风,在我心头弹奏漪澜的乐音。

12

"WHAT language is thine, O sea?"
"The language of eternal question."
"What language is thy answer, O sky?"
"The language of eternal silence."

"你用什么语言说话,大海?"

"永恒追问的语言。"

"你用什么语言作答,天空?"

"永恒沉默的语言。"

13

LISTEN, my heart, to the whispers of the world with which it makes love to you.

听着那些絮语,我的心,世界以此与你欢娱。

14

THE mystery of creation is like the darkness of night—it is great. Delusions of knowledge are like the fog of the morning.

创造的神秘犹如夜的黑暗——何其伟大。知识的错觉好比晨雾。

15

DO not seat your love upon a precipice because it is high.

别因为高耸就把你的爱安放在峭壁。

16

I SIT at my window this morning where the world like a passer—by stops for a moment, nods to me and goes.

清晨,我坐在窗前,世界像一个过客稍事停留,朝我点点头又离去。

17

THESE little thoughts are the rustle of leaves; they have their whisper of joy in my mind.

这些小小的思绪,是叶子的窸窣;它们将喜悦的呢喃放进我的心里。

18

WHAT you are you do not see, what you see is your shadow.

真实的你,你看不见;你看见的,是你的影子。

19

MY wishes are fools, they shout across thy songs, my Master.

Let me but listen.

我的心愿是些傻瓜,它们隔着您的歌呼喊,我的主人。

且让我倾听。

20

I CANNOT choose the best.

The best chooses me.

我无法选择最好的。

那最好的选择我。

21

THEY throw their shadows before them who carry their lantern on their back.

背负着灯的人,将影子投到自己的身前。

22

THAT I exist is a perpetual surprise which is life.

我存活于世是一个持续的惊喜,叫作人生。

23

"WE, the rustling leaves, have a voice that answers the storms, but who are you so silent?"
"I am a mere flower."

"我们,这些窸窸窣窣的叶子,拥有应答暴风雨的声音,可如此沉默的你是谁?"
"我不过是一朵花。"

24

REST belongs to the work as the eyelids to the eyes.

休息属于工作,就像眼睑属于眼睛。

25

MAN is a born child, his power is the power of growth.

成人天生就是孩子,他的力量是成长的力量。

26

GOD expects answers for the flowers he sends us, not for the sun and the earth.

上帝期待我们回报的,是他赠给我们的鲜花,而非太阳和大地。

27

THE light that plays, like a naked child, among the green leaves happily knows not that man can lie.

绿叶间嬉戏的光,赤裸孩童般欢乐,并不知道人会撒谎。

28

O BEAUTY, find thyself in love, not in the flattery of thy mirror.

美啊,你要在爱里找到自己,而非镜子的逢迎里。

29

MY heart beats her waves at the shore of the world and writes upon it her signature in tears with the words, "I love thee."

我的心潮拍打着世界的岸边,在那里含泪用三个字作为自己的签名:我爱你。

30

"MOON, for what do you wait?"
"To salute the sun for whom I must make way."

"月儿,你在等待什么?"
"向我必须让路的太阳敬礼。"

31

THE trees come up to my window like the yearning voice of the dumb earth.

树木簇拥到我的窗前,一如喑哑大地那焦渴的嗓音。

32

HIS own mornings are new surprises to God.

对上帝而言,他自己的一个个清晨,是一个个新的惊喜。

33

LIFE finds its wealth by the claims of the world, and its worth by the claims of love.

生命以拥有世界找到财富,拥有爱找到价值。

34

THE dry river-bed finds no thanks for its past.

干涸的河床对它的过去毫无好感。

35

THE bird wishes it were a cloud. The cloud wishes it were a bird.

鸟愿自己是朵云。云愿自己是只鸟。

36

THE waterfall sings, "I find my song, when I find my freedom."

瀑布唱着:"当我找到我的自由,我就找到了我的歌。"

37

I CANNOT tell why this heart languishes in silence.
It is for small needs it never asks, or knows or remembers.

我说不清这颗心何以默默饱受煎熬。

是为着它从不会开口,不会知晓,不会记得的小小需求。

38

WOMAN, when you move about in your household service your limbs sing like a hill stream among its pebbles.

女人,当你走来走去做着家务,你的肢体像山溪在卵石间欢歌。

39

THE sun goes to cross the Western sea, leaving its last salutation to the East.

太阳前去跨越西方的海洋,将最后的敬礼留给东方。

40

DO not blame your food because you have no appetite.

别因为没有胃口而去责备食物。

41

THE trees, like the longings of the earth, stand a-tiptoe to peep at the heaven.

树就像大地的种种渴望,纷纷踮起脚尖窥探天堂。

42

YOU smiled and talked to me of nothing and I felt that for this I had been waiting long.

你笑了,什么也没对我说,我却感到为了这,我等了很久很久。

43

THE fish in the water is silent, the animal on the earth is noisy, the bird in the air is singing.

But Man has in him the silence of the sea, the noise of the earth and the music of the air.

鱼在水里沉默,兽在地上喧噪,空中的鸟儿唱着歌。

人的心里有海的沉默、大地的喧嚣和空中的音乐。

44

THE world rushes on over the strings of the lingering heart making the music of sadness.

世界匆匆向前,拨动缠绵的心上根根丝弦,奏出悲伤的曲子。

45

HE has made his weapons his gods. When his weapons win he is defeated himself.

他将武器当作他的上帝。当他的武器赢了,他自己就给打败了。

46

GOD finds himself by creating.

上帝在创造中发现自己。

47

SHADOW, with her veil drawn, follows Light in secret meekness, with her silent steps of love.

面纱既垂,影子秘密而顺从地跟随着光,踏着无声的爱的步子。

48

THE stars are not afraid to appear like fireflies.

星星并不担心看上去像萤火虫。

49

I THANK thee that I am none of the wheels of power but I am one with the living creatures that are crushed by it.

我要感激您让我根本不是什么权力的轮子,可我与为权力轮子所碾碎的众生成为一体。

50

THE mind, sharp but not broad, sticks at every point but does not move.

头脑，若敏锐而不宽阔，便缠结于每一个论点，动弹不得。

51

YOUR idol is shattered in the dust to prove that God's dust is greater than your idol.

你的偶像在尘土中碎成齑粉，恰恰证明上帝的尘土比你的偶像伟大。

52

MAN does not reveal himself in his history, he struggles up through it.

人不会在历史中自我显现，他在历史中挣扎着露出头脚。

53

WHILE the glass lamp rebukes the earthen for calling it cousin, the moon rises, and the glass lamp, with a bland smile, calls her, "My dear, dear sister."

正当玻璃灯呵斥陶灯跟自己攀亲沾故,月亮升起来了,玻璃灯赶忙笑吟吟地喊道:"我亲亲、亲亲的姐妹。"

54

LIKE the meeting of the seagulls and the waves we meet and come near. The seagulls fly off, the waves roll away and we depart.

一如海鸥与海浪的相会,我们见面,靠近。海鸥飞走了,海浪退去,我们作别。

55

MY day is done, and I am like a boat drawn on the beach, listening to the dance-music of the tide in the evening.

我的一日过完了,我就像一艘被拖上岸的船,倾听晚潮的舞曲。

56

LIFE is given to us, we earn it by giving it.

生命赐给了我们，我们付出生命赢得人生。

57

WE come nearest to the great when we are great in humility.

当我们在卑微中做到高贵，我们便最接近高贵。

58

THE sparrow is sorry for the peacock at the burden of its tail.

麻雀怜惜孔雀要背着尾巴的重负。

59

NEVER be afraid of the moments——thus sings the voice of the everlasting.

千万不要惧怕一时——永恒用它的歌声如是唱道。

60

THE hurricane seeks the shortest road by the no-road, and suddenly ends its search in the Nowhere.

飓风借无路寻求最短的路,在乌有乡猝然终止搜寻。

61

TAKE my wine in my own cup, friend.

It loses its wreath of foam when poured into that of others.

在我自己的杯里饮我的酒吧,朋友。

一旦倒入别人的杯子,便失去了酒沫的花环。

62

THE Perfect decks itself in beauty for the love of the Imperfect.

完满怀着对不完满的爱,用美装扮自己。

63

GOD says to man, "I heal you therefore I hurt, love you therefore punish."

上帝对人说:"我疗治你,因此我伤害;爱你,因此我惩罚。"

64

THANK the flame for its light, but do not forget the lampholder standing in the shade with constancy of patience.

感激火焰带来光明,但不可忘记以持久的耐心站在暗处的掌灯人。

65

TINY grass, your steps are small, but you possess the earth under your tread.

小小的青草,你脚步虽小,却拥有足下的土地。

66

THE infant flower opens its bud and cries, "Dear World, please do not fade."

幼小的花朵张开花蕾,喊道:"亲爱的世界,请别枯萎。"

67

GOD grows weary of great kingdoms, but never of little flowers.

上帝会厌倦伟大的王国,但绝不会厌倦微小的花朵。

68

WRONG cannot afford defeat but Right can.

错经不起失败,对却经得起。

69

"I GIVE my whole water in joy," sings the waterfall, "though little of it is enough for the thirsty."

"我欣欣地给出了我全部的水,"瀑布唱道,"尽管一丁点儿就足以止渴。"

70

WHERE is the fountain that throws up these flowers in a ceaseless outbreak of ecstasy?

以无休无止喷涌的狂喜举起这些花朵的喷泉,你的源泉在哪里?

71

THE woodcutter's axe begged for its handle from the tree.

The tree gave it.

樵夫的斧子向树乞要斧柄。

树给了它。

72

IN my solitude of heart I feel the sigh of this widowed evening veiled with mist and rain.

这守寡的黄昏,披着雨雾的面纱,我在心的孤寂中感觉到了她的叹息。

73

CHASTITY is a wealth that comes from abundance of love.

贞操是财富,源自爱的丰饶。

74

THE mist, like love, plays upon the heart of the hills and brings out surprises of beauty.

雾霭,像爱一样,撩拨着群山的心,带来种种美的惊喜。

75

WE read the world wrong and say that it deceives us.

我们错会了世界,说世界欺骗了我们。

76

THE poet wind is out over the sea and the forest to seek his own voice.

作为诗人的风在大海和森林漫卷,寻找自己的声音。

77

EVERY child comes with the message that God is not yet discouraged of man.

每一个孩子都带来口信:上帝对人类还没灰心。

78

THE grass seeks her crowd in the earth.
The tree seeks his solitude of the sky.

小草在地上寻觅伙伴。
树向天空离群索居。

79

MAN barricades against himself.

人类设置路障对抗自己。

80

YOUR voice, my friend, wanders in my heart, like the muffled sound of the sea among these listening pines.

你的声音,朋友,在我心中游荡,恰似这倾听着的苍松间压低的海涛声。

81

WHAT is this unseen flame of darkness whose sparks are the stars?

这看不见的黑暗火焰是什么——星星是它的火花?

82

LET life be beautiful like summer flowers and death like autumn leaves.

要生如夏花般绚烂,死若秋叶般静美。

83

HE who wants to do good knocks at the gate; he who loves finds the gate open.

欲做好人者,在门口敲门;爱人在心者,见门敞开着。

84

IN death the many becomes one; in life the one becomes many. Religion will be one when God is dead.

死后,万人是一人;生时,一人是万人。
上帝一死,世间便只有一种宗教。

85

THE artist is the lover of Nature, therefore he is her slave and her master.

艺术家是大自然的情人,因此是她的奴仆和主人。

86

"HOW far are you from me, O Fruit?"
"I am hidden in your heart, O Flower."

"你离我有多远呢,果实?"
"我就藏在你的心里呀,花朵。"

87

THIS longing is for the one who is felt in the dark, but not seen in the day.

这渴望的对象,是那在黑夜里体会到,而非白日里看到的人。

88

"YOU are the big drop of dew under the lotus leaf, I am the smaller one on its upper side," said the dewdrop to the lake.

"你是荷叶底下那颗硕大的露珠,我是叶子上面小得多的那滴。"露珠对湖水说。

89

THE scabbard is content to be dull when it protects the keenness of the sword.

保护了宝剑的锋利,剑鞘乐守其钝。

90

IN darkness the One appears as uniform; in the light the One appears as manifold.

黑暗里,一显得整齐划一;光亮处,一显得斑驳陆离。

91

THE great earth makes herself hospitable with the help of the grass.

有了青草，大地变得殷勤可人。

92

THE birth and death of the leaves are the rapid whirls of the eddy whose wider circles move slowly among stars.

叶子的生生死死，是旋涡的飞旋，它那更宽广的波轮在星辰间缓慢移动。

93

POWER said to the world, "You are mine."
The world kept it prisoner on her throne.
Love said to the world, "I am thine."
The world gave it the freedom of her house.

权力对世界说："你属于我。"
世界将它扣在宝座上做囚徒。
爱对世界说："我属于您。"
世界还之以自由使用她屋宇的权利。

94

THE mist is like the earth's desire. It hides the sun for whom she cries.

雾就像大地的欲望。它隐藏起大地所哭求的太阳。

95

BE still, my heart, these great trees are prayers.

安静,我的心,这些硕大的树是在做祷告的。

96

THE noise of the moment scoffs at the music of the Eternal.

一时的噪音嘲笑永恒的音乐。

97

I THINK of other ages that floated upon the stream of life and love and death and are forgotten, and I feel the freedom of passing away.

想到另一些浮荡在生死情爱溪河之上已然被忘却的岁月,我感到消逝的自由自在。

98

THE sadness of my soul is her bride's veil.
It waits to be lifted in the night.

我灵魂的这份悲伤是她的婚纱。

等待着夜间揭去。

99

DEATH'S stamp gives value to the coin of life; making it possible to buy with life what is truly precious.

死亡的印戳赋值于人生这枚硬币,使之得以用生命买到真正珍贵的东西。

100

THE cloud stood humbly in a corner of the sky.
The morning crowned it with splendour.

云朵卑微地站在天空一角。

清晨给它戴上壮丽的皇冠。

101

THE dust receives insult and in return offers her flowers.

尘土受到侮辱,却报之以鲜花。

102

DO not linger to gather flowers to keep them, but walk on, for flowers will keep themselves blooming all your way.

不要为着留住鲜花而逗留采撷,往前走,鲜花会随着你一路盛开。

103

ROOTS are the branches down in the earth.
Branches are roots in the air.

根须是深入大地的枝丫。
枝丫是伸到空中的根须。

104

THE music of the far-away summer flutters around the Autumn seeking its former nest.

遥远夏日的音乐,在秋的周遭扑腾,寻觅从前的窠巢。

105

DO not insult your friend by lending him merits from your own pocket.

不要从自己的口袋把荣誉借给朋友,那是侮辱他。

106

THE touch of the nameless days clings to my heart like mosses round the old tree.

那些莫名的日子揪着我的心,挥拂不去,就像老树身上裹着的苔藓。

107

THE echo mocks her origin to prove she is the original.

回声嘲讽她的源头,以证明她是原声。

108

GOD is ashamed when the prosperous boasts of His special favour.

上帝羞于听见发达的人吹嘘得了他特别的恩惠。

109

I CAST my own shadow upon my path, because I have a lamp that has not been lighted.

我将自己的影子投在路上,因为我有一盏尚未点着的灯。

110

MAN goes into the noisy crowd to drown his own clamour of silence.

人到喧闹的人群中,去淹没自己默默的抗议。

111

THAT which ends in exhaustion is death, but the perfect ending is in the endless.

以竭而终者谓之死,善终却止于无止无终。

112

THE sun has his simple robe of light.
The clouds are decked with gorgeousness.

太阳披着简朴的光袍。

云朵拥有华丽的衣装。

113

THE hills are like shouts of children who raise their arms, trying to catch stars.

群山就像孩童在呼喊,他们举起臂膀,试图捉住星星。

114

THE road is lonely in its crowd for it is not loved.

那条路因不被喜爱而在众路中寂寞着。

115

THE power that boasts of its mischiefs is laughed at by the yellow leaves that fall, and clouds that pass by.

夸耀自己累累恶行的权力,取笑它的,有飘落的黄叶、飞逝的云朵。

116

THE earth hums to me to-day in the sun, like a woman at her spinning, some ballad of the ancient time in a forgotten tongue.

今天的大地，在阳光下，像正在纺纱的妇人，用早被遗忘的语言，对我哼着某首远古的谣曲。

117

THE grass-blade is worth of the great world where it grows.

草叶无愧于它生长的大千世界。

118

DREAM is a wife who must talk.
Sleep is a husband who silently suffers.

梦是喋喋不休的妻子。
睡是默默忍受的丈夫。

119

THE night kisses the fading day whispering to his ear, "I am death, your mother. I am to give you fresh birth."

夜亲吻消退的白昼,悄声耳语道:"我是死,你的母亲。我就要给你新生。"

120

I FEEL, thy beauty, dark night, like that of the loved woman when she has put out the lamp.

黑夜,我感受到了你的美,美得恰似一位怜爱的女人在她熄灯之后。

121

I CARRY in my world that flourishes the worlds that have failed.

我在我功成名就的世界里,背负着多少功败垂成的世界。

122

DEAR friend, I feel the silence of your great thoughts of many a deepening eventide on this beach when I listen to these waves.

亲爱的朋友,当我在此海滩倾听涛声,好几次,渐深的薄暮勾起你翻腾的思绪,我感受着它们的沉默。

123

THE bird thinks it is an act of kindness to give the fish a lift in the air.

鸟儿将鱼儿提携到空中,以为那是一个善举。

124

"IN the moon thou sendest thy love letters to me," said the night to the sun.

"I leave my answers in tears upon the grass."

"月光下,您将情书寄给我。"夜对太阳说。

"我将我含泪的回答留在青草上。"

125

THE Great is a born child; when he dies he gives his great childhood to the world.

伟人是天生的孩子;死时他将他伟大的童年留给世界。

126

NOT hammerstrokes, but dance of the water sings the pebbles into perfection.

将卵石唱得珠圆玉润的,是水的舞曲,而非丁丁锤声。

127

BEES sip honey from flowers and hum their thanks when they leave.

The gaudy butterfly is sure that the flowers owe thanks to him.

蜜蜂从花丛嘬蜜,离去时哼着感激的曲子。

华而不实的蝴蝶认定花儿该感激他。

128

TO be outspoken is easy when you do not wait to speak the complete truth.

直言不讳是容易的,若你等不到说出全部实情。

129

ASKS the Possible to the Impossible, "Where is your dwelling place?"

"In the dreams of the impotent," comes the answer.

"可能的"问"不可能的":"哪里是你的居所?"

"在无能者的梦里。"这便是回答。

130

IF you shut your door to all errors truth will be shut out.

倘若你对所有的错误关上门,真理便被关在了门外。

131

I HEAR some rustle of things behind my sadness of heart,—I cannot see them.

我听见什么在我心的悲伤后面窸窸窣窣——我看不见它们。

132

LEISURE in its activity is work.
The stillness of the sea stirs in waves.

活动着的休闲,就是工作。
海的平静激荡波涛。

133

THE leaf becomes flower when it loves.
The flower becomes fruit when it worships.

叶子爱时,成为花朵。
花朵崇拜,便成果实。

134

THE roots below the earth claim no rewards for making the branches fruitful.

地下的根须,不因让枝丫硕果累累而索求回报。

135

THIS rainy evening the wind is restless.

I look at the swaying branches and ponder over the greatness of all things.

这雨纷纷的黄昏,风躁动不宁。

望着摇曳的树枝,我思索万物何以伟大。

136

STORM of midnight, like a giant child awakened in the untimely dark, has begun to play and shout.

子夜的风暴,恰似黑地里不合时宜惊醒的巨婴,开始又哭又闹。

137

THOU raisest thy waves vainly to follow thy lover. O sea, thou lonely bride of the storm.

你掀起波涛徒劳地追赶你的情人。啊,大海,你这暴风雨孑然的新娘。

138

"I AM ashamed of my emptiness," said the Word to the Work.

"I know how poor I am when I see you," said the Work to the Word.

"我羞愧于我的空洞。"词语对作品说。

"见到你,我知道了我多么寒碜。"作品对词语说。

139

TIME is the wealth of change, but the clock in its parody makes it mere change and no wealth.

时间是变化的财富,拙劣模仿的时钟只宣告变化而不带来财富。

140

TRUTH in her dress finds facts too tight.
In fiction she moves with ease.

真实穿上衣服便觉事实紧得难受。

在虚构中她游刃有余。

141

WHEN I travelled to here and to there, I was tired of thee, O Road, but now when thou leadest me to everywhere I am wedded to thee in love.

当我四处奔波,我厌倦了你,路啊,可如今当你让我四通八达,我和你结为爱的连理。

142

LET me think that there is one among those stars that guides my life through the dark unknown.

我且以为,那些星星中有一颗指引我的人生穿过黑暗的未知。

143

WOMAN, with the grace of your fingers you touched my things and order came out like music.

女人,蒙你手指之恩,你碰过我的东西,一切便如音乐般井然有序。

144

ONE sad voice has its nest among the ruins of the years.
It sings to me in the night,— "I loved you."

一个凄苦的声音筑窠在岁月的废墟里。
夜里它对我唱道:"我爱过你。"

145

THE flaming fire warns me off by its own glow.
Save me from the dying embers hidden under ashes.

熊熊的烈火以火焰警告我离开。
救我于隐藏在灰烬下奄奄一息的余火吧。

146

I HAVE my stars in the sky,
But oh for my little lamp unlit in my house.

我有星星在天空,

哦,我屋子里小小的灯盏却尚未点燃。

147

THE dust of the dead words clings to thee.
Wash thy soul with silence.

僵死词语的尘屑粘在你身上。

用无言洗净你的灵魂。

148

GAPS are left in life through which comes the sad music of death.

生命一旦留下缝隙,死神悲伤的乐音便从中流出。

149

THE world has opened its heart of light in the morning. Come out, my heart, with thy love to meet it.

世界在清晨敞开它光明的心。

出来呀,我的心,用你的爱去迎接。

150

MY thoughts shimmer with these shimmering leaves and my heart sings with the touch of this sunlight; my life is glad to be floating with all things into the blue of space, into the dark of time.

因着这些闪光的叶子,我的思绪闪闪发光,因着这阳光的轻抚,我的心歌唱;与万物一同悠然飘进空间的蔚蓝、时间的黑暗,我的人生不亦快哉。

151

GOD'S great power is in the gentle breeze, not in the storm.

上帝的伟力,见于轻风,而非风暴。

152

THIS is a dream in which things are all loose and they oppress. I shall find them gathered in thee when I awake and shall be free.

在这样一个梦里,万物散乱不羁,压在心头。醒来时,我将发觉一切归聚于您,于是悠游自在。

153

"WHO is there to take up my duties?" asked the setting sun.

"I shall do what I can, my Master," said the earthen lamp.

"你们谁来接下我的职责?"夕阳问。

"我将尽我所能,主人。"陶灯说道。

154

BY plucking her petals you do not gather the beauty of the flower.

摘花的瓣儿,采不到花的美。

155

SILENCE will carry your voice like the nest that holds the sleeping birds.

沉默承载着你的声音，恰似鸟窝托护着熟睡的鸟儿。

156

THE Great walks with the Small without fear.
The Middling keeps aloof.

伟大与渺小并肩而行，彼此毫无惧色。
中不溜儿却格格不入。

157

THE night opens the flowers in secret and allows the day to get thanks.

夜悄悄打开花朵，让白昼收得感谢。

158

POWER takes as ingratitude the writhings of its victims.

权力将它的受害者的痛恶视作忘恩负义。

159

WHEN we rejoice in our fulness, then we can part with our fruits with joy.

当我们因自己的充实而喜悦,我们便能欢喜地告别我们的果实。

160

THE raindrops kissed the earth and whispered,— "We are thy homesick children, mother, come back to thee from the heaven."

雨滴亲吻大地,喃喃低语:"我们是您思乡的孩子,母亲,从天上回到您身边。"

161

THE cobweb pretends to catch dew-drops and catches flies.

蛛网假装捕捉露珠,捉住了苍蝇。

162

LOVE! when you come with the burning lamp of pain in your hand, I can see your face and know you as bliss.

爱！当你手举痛苦煎熬的油灯走来，我从你的脸上看出你就是极乐。

163

"THE learned say that your lights will one day be no more." said the firefly to the stars.

The stars made no answer.

"有学问的人说，你们的光总有一天不再有。"萤火虫对天上的星星说。

星星不予回答。

164

IN the dusk of the evening the bird of some early dawn comes to the nest of my silence.

在黄昏的薄暮里，某只黎明早起的鸟儿来到我的沉默之窠。

165

THOUGHTS pass in my mind like flocks of ducks in the sky.

I hear the voice of their wings.

思绪掠过我的脑际,恰似鸭群飞过天空。

我听见它们振翅的声音。

166

THE canal loves to think that rivers exist solely to supply it with water.

运河总爱以为河流的存在,只是为它供水。

167

THE world has kissed my soul with its pain, asking for its return in songs.

世界用痛苦亲吻我的灵魂,却要以歌声作为回报。

168

THAT which oppresses me, is it my soul trying to come out in the open, or the soul of the world knocking at my heart for its entrance?

那折磨着我的,是我的灵魂在竭力逃到外面的旷野,还是世界的灵魂在叩击我的心门要进来?

169

THOUGHT feeds itself with its own words and grows.

思想以自己的词语喂养自己成长。

170

I HAVE dipped the vessel of my heart into this silent hour; it has filled with love.

我把心的容器浸入这静默的时刻;它注满了爱。

171

EITHER you have work or you have not.

When you have to say, "Let us do something," then begins mischief.

你要么有事做，要么没有。

当你不得不说"让我们做点什么吧"，祸害便开始了。

172

THE sunflower blushed to own the nameless flower as her kin.

The sun rose and smiled on it, saying, "Are you well, my darling?"

向日葵羞于有无名花做她的亲戚。

太阳升起，笑着对无名花说："你还好吗，我的亲亲？"

173

"WHO drives me forward like fate?"
"The Myself striding on my back."

"是谁像命运似的驱使我向前？"

"那个在我背上阔步前进的自我。"

174

THE clouds fill the watercups of the river, hiding themselves in the distant hills.

云朵灌满河流的水杯,藏身于远山。

175

I SPILL water from my water jar as I walk on my way, Very little remains for my home.

我一路上泼洒水罐里的水,

只剩寥寥几滴带回家。

176

THE water in a vessel is sparkling; the water in the sea is dark.

The small truth has words that are clear; the great truth has great silence.

杯子里的水闪闪发光;海里的水一片黑暗。

小真理言语响亮;大真理大沉默。

177

YOUR smile was the flowers of your own fields, your talk was the rustle of your own mountain pines, but your heart was the woman that we all know.

你的微笑是你自己田地里的花朵,你的谈话是你自己山上松林的窸窣,而你的心却是我们全都认识的那个女人。

178

IT is the little things that I leave behind for my loved ones,—great things are for everyone.

我留给至亲的,是些微之物——好东西要给大家。

179

WOMAN, thou hast encircled the world's heart with the depth of thy tears as the sea has the earth.

女人,你以你泪水的深渊包围着世界的心,恰似大海包围着陆地。

180

THE sunshine greets me with a smile. The rain, his sad sister, talks to my heart.

阳光用微笑迎接我。雨，它伤心的妹妹，跟我的心说话。

181

MY flower of the day dropped its petals forgotten.
In the evening it ripens into a golden fruit of memory.

我白日的花朵掉下被人遗忘的花瓣。
夜里，它成熟了，结出一枚记忆的金果。

182

I AM like the road in the night listening to the footfalls of its memories in silence.

我就像夜里的道路，默默倾听记忆的脚步声。

183

THE evening sky to me is like a window, and a lighted lamp, and a waiting behind it.

黄昏的天空,在我眼里,就像一扇窗,一盏点亮的灯,灯后的一次等待。

184

HE who is too busy doing good finds no time to be good.

太忙于行善之人,到头来却没有时间做个善人。

185

I AM the autumn cloud, empty of rain, see my fulness in the field of ripened rice.

我是那秋天的云,空空无雨,到稻子熟透的田里去看我的丰盈吧。

186

THEY hated and killed and men praised them.

But God in shame hastens to hide its memory under the green grass.

他们恨,他们杀戮,人们赞美他们。

上帝羞愧得匆匆将那段记忆掩埋在青草之下。

187

TOES are the fingers that have forsaken their past.

脚趾是遗弃了过去的手指。

188

DARKNESS travels towards light, but blindness towards death.

黑暗走向光明,盲目则走向死亡。

189

THE pet dog suspects the universe for scheming to take its place.

宠物犬疑心宇宙算计着要取代它的位置。

190

SIT still my heart, do not raise your dust.
Let the world find its way to you.

坐稳了,我的心,别掀起你的尘埃。
让世界设法找到你。

191

THE bow whispers to the arrow before it speeds forth—
"Your freedom is mine."

发射之前,弓对箭悄声低语:"你的自由是我的。"

192

WOMAN, in your laughter you have the music of the fountain of life.

女人,你的欢笑声里流淌着生命之泉的乐音。

193

A MIND all logic is like a knife all blade.
It makes the hand bleed that uses it.

一个全是逻辑的头脑,就像一把全是锋刃的刀。
只会让用它的手流血。

194

GOD loves man's lamp lights better than his own great stars.

上帝爱人间的灯光,胜过自己巨大的星星。

195

THIS world is the world of wild storms kept tame with the music of beauty.

这个世界,是被美的乐曲所驯服的狂风暴雨的世界。

196

"MY heart is like the golden casket of thy kiss," said the sunset cloud to the sun.

"我的心,就像装您亲吻的金色宝箱。"晚霞对夕阳说。

197

BY touching you may kill, by keeping away you may possess.

爱抚未必不会杀害，远离也许就会拥有。

198

THE cricket's chirp and the patter of rain come to me through the dark, like the rustle of dreams from my past youth.

蛩鸣和着雨点穿过黑夜来到我枕边，就像我逝去青春的梦窸窸窣窣。

199

"I HAVE lost my dewdrop," cries the flower to the morning sky that has lost all its stars.

"我失去了我的露珠。"鲜花对着已然失去所有星星的晨空嚷道。

200

THE burning log bursts in flame and cries,— "This is my flower, my death."

燃烧的木头猛然绽开烈焰,哭喊:"这是我的花朵,我的死。"

201

THE wasp thinks that the honey-hive of the neighbouring bees is too small.

His neighbours ask him to build one still smaller.

黄蜂觉得邻居蜜蜂的蜂巢太小。

邻居要他造出一个更小的来。

202

"I CANNOT keep your waves," says the bank to the river.

"Let me keep your footprints in my heart."

"我留不住你的波浪。"岸对河说。

"让我把你的足迹留在心里。"

203

THE day, with the noise of this little earth, drowns the silence of all worlds.

白昼,以这小小地球的喧嚣,淹没了所有天体的静默。

204

THE song feels the infinite in the air, the picture in the earth, the poem in the air and the earth;

For its words have meaning that walks and music that soars.

歌在天空感受到了无穷,图画的无穷在大地上,诗的无穷在天空和大地;

因为它的词语既有行走的意义,又有翱翔乐音。

205

WHEN the sun goes down to the West, the East of his morning stands before him in silence.

当太阳到西边落下,他清晨的东方默默站在他的面前。

206

LET me not put myself wrongly to my world and set it against me.

我可别把自己错呈给了世界,让世界反对我。

207

PRAISE shames me, for I secretly beg for it.

赞美让我蒙羞,因为我偷偷把它乞求。

208

LET my doing nothing when I have nothing to do become untroubled in its depth of peace like the evening in the seashore when the water is silent.

当我无所事事时,就让我的无所事事在宁静的深邃里不受纷扰,一如海水静默时海边的黄昏。

209

MAIDEN, your simplicity, like the blueness of the lake, reveals your depth of truth.

少女,你的朴素,恰似湖水的湛蓝,显露出你纯真的深度。

210

THE best does not come alone.
It comes with the company of the all.

最好的,并非单独而来。
它受到万众簇拥。

211

GOD'S right hand is gentle, but terrible is his left hand.

上帝的右手温婉,左手却无比可怕。

212

MY evening came among the alien trees and spoke in a language which my morning stars did not know.

我的黄昏来到异乡的树林,说着一种我的晨星听不懂的语言。

213

NIGHT'S darkness is a bag that bursts with the gold of the dawn.

夜的黑暗,是一只被黎明的金子撑破的布袋。

214

OUR desire lends the colours of the rainbow to the mere mists and vapours of life.

我们的欲望,将彩虹的色彩赋予那只不过是迷雾与泡影的人生。

215

GOD waits to win back his own flowers as gifts from man's hands.

上帝等着从人类手里赢回自己作为礼物的鲜花。

216

MY sad thoughts tease me asking me their own names.

我悲伤的思绪取笑我,问我它们自己的名字。

217

THE service of the fruit is precious, the service of the flower is sweet, but let my service be the service of the leaves in its shade of humble devotion.

果实之用珍贵,花朵之用甜美,就让我之用成为叶子之用,以卑微的奉献垂下树荫。

218

MY heart has spread its sails to the idle winds for the shadowy island of Anywhere.

我的心已对懒散的风张开帆,去寻找那叫作"无论何地"的幻岛。

219

MEN are cruel, but Man is kind.

众人虽残忍,个人本善良。

220

MAKE me thy cup and let my fulness be for thee and for thine.

把我做成您的杯子,让我的丰满服务于您和您的一切。

221

THE storm is like the cry of some god in pain whose love the earth refuses.

风暴就像某个神痛苦中的哭喊,他的爱被大地所拒绝。

222

THE world does not leak because death is not a crack.

世界不会漏掉,因为死亡不是一个裂隙。

223

LIFE has become richer by the love that has been lost.

人生因失去的爱而变得更加丰富。

224

MY friend, your great heart shone with the sunrise of the East like the snowy summit of a lonely hill in the dawn.

我的朋友,你伟大的心脏因东方的旭日而闪耀,恰似曙光里一座孤山的雪顶。

225

THE fountain of death makes the still water of life play.

死亡之泉让生命的止水流淌起来。

226

THOSE who have everything but thee, my God, laugh at those who have nothing but thyself.

我的上帝,那些除了您什么都拥有的人,嘲笑那些除了您一无所有的人。

227

THE movement of life has its rest in its own music.

生命的运动在它自己的音乐里得到休憩。

228

KICKS only raise dust and not crops from the earth.

跺脚只是扬起大地的灰尘,不会收获庄稼。

229

OUR names are the light that glows on the sea waves at night and then dies without leaving its signature.

我们的名字是夜晚海浪上的光,闪过便消逝,不留下签名。

230

LET him only see the thorns who has eyes to see the rose.

有眼力鉴赏玫瑰的人,就让他只看见刺吧。

231

SET bird's wings with gold and it will never again soar in the sky.

用金子装点鸟的翅膀,它再也不会在天空翱翔。

232

THE same lotus of our clime blooms here in the alien water with the same sweetness, under another name.

我们气候区的莲,在这异乡的水里开放,有着一样的馨香,不一样的名字。

233

IN heart's perspective the distance looms large.

在心的视野里,距离悚然变大。

234

THE moon has her light all over the sky, her dark spots to herself.

月亮将辉光洒满天空,把暗影留给自己。

235

DO not say, "It is morning," and dismiss it with a name of yesterday. See it for the first time as a new-born child that has no name.

不要说"早晨了",就用一个昨天的名字把它打发。要像头一回见到还没名字的新生儿那般看待它。

236

SMOKE boasts to the sky, and Ashes to the earth, that they are brothers to the fire.

烟雾对天空吹嘘,灰烬对大地吹嘘,说它们是火的兄弟。

237

THE raindrop whispered to the jasmine, "Keep me in your heart for ever."

The jasmine sighed, "Alas," and dropped to the ground.

雨滴对茉莉私语:"把我永远留在你的心里。"

茉莉"唉"一声叹口气,便掉落在地。

238

TIMID thoughts, do not be afraid of me.

I am a poet.

腼腆的思绪,别怕我。

我是诗人。

239

THE dim silence of my mind seems filled with crickets' chirp—the grey twilight of sound.

我心里隐约的静寂,仿佛充满着蛩鸣——那如灰色暮光般的声响。

240

ROCKETS, your insult to the stars follows yourself back to the earth.

烟花哟,你对星辰的侮辱又跟着你自己回到了地球。

241

THOU hast led me through my crowded travels of the day to my evening's loneliness.

I wait for its meaning through the stillness of the night.

您领着我穿过白昼挤挤挨挨的旅程抵达夜晚的孤寂。

透过夜的静谧,我等候它的意义。

242

THIS life is the crossing of a sea, where we meet in the same narrow ship.

In death we reach the shore and go to our different worlds.

这一生,是漂洋过海,我们相遇在同一条舴艋舟。

死时,我们抵达彼岸,然后走向各自不同的世界。

243

THE stream of truth flows through its channels of mistakes.

真理的溪河流过它错误的沟沟渠渠。

244

MY heart is homesick to-day for the one sweet hour across the sea of time.

今朝,我的心思念时光之海彼岸那甜美的一刻。

245

THE bird-song is the echo of the morning light back from the earth.

鸟歌,是大地上晨光的回声。

246

"ARE you too proud to kiss me?" the morning light asks the buttercup.

"你是不是傲骄得不肯吻我?"晨光问毛茛。

247

"HOW may I sing to thee and worship, O Sun?" asked the little flower.

"By the simple silence of thy purity," answered the sun.

"我该怎样歌唱您、崇拜您,哦,太阳?"小花问道。

"就以你的那纯洁质朴的无言吧。"太阳回道。

248

MAN is worse than an animal when he is an animal.

人一旦成了畜生,便不如畜生。

249

DARK clouds become heaven's flowers when kissed by light.

乌云一旦被光亲吻,便成为天堂的花朵。

250

LET not the sword-blade mock its handle for being blunt.

可别让剑刃嘲笑剑柄钝而无能。

251

THE night's silence, like a deep lamp, is burning with the light of its milky way.

夜的寂静,就像一盏深灯,燃的是银河的光。

252

AROUND the sunny island of Life swells day and night death's limitless song of the sea.

在阳光明媚的生之岛的周遭,大海日夜涌动着死神无穷无尽的歌。

253

IS not this mountain like a flower, with its petals of hills, drinking the sunlight?

难道这座山不像一朵花?它群峰的花瓣啜饮着阳光。

254

THE real with its meaning read wrong and emphasis misplaced is the unreal.

真实,一旦给会错意、落错重点,便成为不真实。

255

FIND your beauty, my heart, from the world's movement, like the boat that has the grace of the wind and the water.

从世界的律动中发现你的美吧,我的心,就像享受顺风顺水之恩的行舟。

256

THE eyes are not proud of their sight but of their eyeglasses.

眼睛不以视力为自豪,却以眼镜为傲。

257

I LIVE in this little world of mine and am afraid to make it the least less. Lift me into thy world and let me have the freedom gladly to lose my all.

我活在自己这小小的世界,生恐失去哪怕一点点。将我提携到您的世界吧,让我享受那份自在,快乐地失去自己的一切。

258

THE false can never grow into truth by growing in power.

假绝不会随着权力的增长而成为真。

259

MY heart, with its lapping waves of song, longs to caress this green world of the sunny day.

我的心,借助它歌声的拍岸波涛,渴望抚慰阳光明媚日子里的这个绿色世界。

260

WAYSIDE grass, love the star, then your dreams will come out in flowers.

路边的野草,爱星星吧,那样你的梦就会开出花朵。

261

LET your music, like a sword, pierce the noise of the market to its heart.

让你的音乐,像利剑,穿透市井的喧嚣直达心里。

262

THE trembling leaves of this tree touch my heart like the fingers of an infant child.

这棵树颤巍巍的叶子像婴儿的手指触动我的心。

263

THE little flower lies in the dust.
It sought the path of the butterfly.

小小的花朵躺在尘埃里。
它寻觅过蝴蝶的路径。

264

I AM in the world of the roads. The night comes. Open thy gate, thou world of the home.

我身处路的世界。夜来了。敞开你的门吧，你家的世界。

265

I HAVE sung the songs of thy day. In the evening let me carry thy lamp through the stormy path.

我已唱过了你白昼的歌。在夜里,让我擎着你的灯,走过暴风雨之路。

266

I DO not ask thee into the house.
Come into my infinite loneliness, my Lover.

我不请你进屋去。
到我无尽的孤寂里来吧,我的爱人。

267

DEATH belongs to life as birth does. The walk is in the raising of the foot as in the laying of it down.

死亡属于生命,一如新生。行走既在步起,也在步落。

268

I HAVE learnt the simple meaning of thy whispers in flowers and sunshine—teach me to know thy words in pain and death.

您花朵与阳光的轻声低语,那单纯的意义我已领会——教给我去懂得您痛苦与死亡的话语吧。

269

THE night's flower was late when the morning kissed her, she shivered and sighed and dropped to the ground.

当早晨亲吻她时,夜之花已然迟暮,她战栗着,叹口气,掉落在地上。

270

THROUGH the sadness of all things I hear the crooning of the Eternal Mother.

透过万物的悲伤,我听见永恒母亲轻哼低吟。

271

I CAME to your shore as a stranger, I lived in your house as a guest, I leave your door as a friend, my earth.

我来到你的岸边是陌生人,住进你的屋子是客人,离开你的家门是朋友,我的大地。

272

LET my thoughts come to you, when I am gone, like the afterglow of sunset at the margin of starry silence.

我离去时,就让我的思念来到你身边,仿佛静默星空边沿那一抹夕阳余晖。

273

LIGHT in my heart the evening star of rest and then let the night whisper to me of love.

点亮我心中那颗休憩晚星,继而让夜对我悄声倾诉爱意。

274

I AM a child in the dark.

I stretch my hands through the coverlet of night for thee, Mother.

我是黑暗中的孩子。

我伸出双手，穿过夜的罩子寻找您，母亲。

275

THE day of work is done. Hide my face in your arms, Mother.

Let me dream.

劳作的白昼终结了。把我的脸藏进你的臂弯，母亲。

让我进入梦乡。

276

THE lamp of meeting burns long; it goes out in a moment at the parting.

相聚的灯燃得长久；它在分别的那一刻熄灭。

277

ONE word keep for me in thy silence, O World, when I am dead, "I have loved."

哦,世界,当我死后,有句话替我留在你的静默里:"我爱过。"

278

WE live in this world when we love it.

当我们爱这个世界,我们便活在世上。

279

LET the dead have the immortality of fame, but the living the immortality of love.

让死者去享受不朽的声名,生者来享受不朽的爱。

280

I HAVE seen thee as the half-awakened child sees his mother in the dusk of the dawn and then smiles and sleeps again.

我看着您,仿佛半睡半醒的孩子看着拂晓幽光里的母亲,笑笑,又睡去。

281

I SHALL die again and again to know that life is inexhaustible.

为懂得生之不竭,我将一次又一次死去。

282

WHILE I was passing with the crowd in the road I saw thy smile from the balcony and I sang and forgot all noise.

当我随着人群路过,我看到你在阳台上微笑,我唱起歌,忘却了所有的喧嚣。

283

LOVE is life in its fulness like the cup with its wine.

爱是完满时的生命,就像盛满酒的杯子。

284

THEY light their own lamps and sing their own words in their temples.

But the birds sing thy name in thine own morning light,—for thy name is joy.

他们点起自己的灯,在自己的寺庙里吟唱他们的词句。

而鸟儿在您自己的晨光里吟唱您的名字,因为您的名字叫欢喜。

285

LEAD me in the centre of thy silence to fill my heart with songs.

把我领到您沉默的中心,好让歌声充满我的心。

286

LET them live who choose in their own hissing world of fireworks.

My heart longs for thy stars, my God.

让他们活在他们自己选定的烟火啸啸世界。

我的心渴望您的星辰,我的上帝。

287

LOVE'S pain sang round my life like the unplumbed sea, and love's joy sang like birds in its flowering groves.

爱之痛苦在我生命的周遭歌唱,仿佛未知深深几许的海;爱之欢喜,却似鸟儿,在鲜花丛中浅唱低吟。

288

PUT out the lamp when thou wishest.
I shall know thy darkness and shall love it.

您愿熄灯且熄灯。
您的黑暗,我将体味我将爱。

289

WHEN I stand before thee at the day's end thou shalt see my scars and know that I had my wounds and also my healing.

当我在人生的尽头站到您的面前,您看到我的疤痕就知道,我伤过,也治愈了。

290

SOME day I shall sing to thee in the sunrise of some other world, "I have seen thee before in the light of the earth, in the love of man."

总有一天,我将在另外某个世界的旭日里对您歌唱:"我从前在大地的光里,在人类的爱里,见过您。"

291

CLOUDS come floating into my life from other days no longer to shed rain or usher storm but to give colour to my sunset sky.

云朵从另外的日子飘进我的人生,不再洒雨,也不引导风暴,只是把色彩带给我那夕阳的天空。

292

TRUTH raises against itself the storm that scatters its seeds broadcast.

真理激起反抗自己的风暴去广为播撒它的种子。

293

THE storm of the last night has crowned this morning with golden peace.

昨夜的暴风雨以金色的宁静加冕了今天的清晨。

294

TRUTH seems to come with its final word; and the final word gives birth to its next.

真理似乎带来结论；结论又诞生下一个。

295

BLESSED is he whose fame does not outshine his truth.

声名不盖实功者有福了。

296

SWEETNESS of thy name fills my heart when I forget mine—like thy morning sun when the mist is melted.

我忘记自己的名字时，您名字的芳馨充满我心——恰似雾霭消融后您的朝阳。

297

THE silent night has the beauty of the mother and the clamorous day of the child.

静谧的夜有着母亲的美,喧闹的白昼有着孩子的美。

298

THE world loved man when he smiled. The world became afraid of him when he laughed.

他微笑时,世界爱他。他大笑时,世界怕他。

299

GOD waits for man to regain his childhood in wisdom.

上帝等着人用智慧重获童年。

300

LET me feel this world as thy love taking form, then my love will help it.

让我在您爱的成形中感受这个世界,好让我的爱能助一臂之力。

301

THY sunshine smiles upon the winter days of my heart, never doubting of its spring flowers.

您的阳光将微笑洒到我心的冬日,从不怀疑它会在春天开花。

302

GOD kisses the finite in his love and man the infinite.

上帝用爱亲吻有限,人亲吻无限。

303

THOU crossest desert lands of barren years to reach the moment of fulfilment.

您穿过荒年的沙漠之地,抵达圆满的时刻。

304

GOD'S silence ripens man's thoughts into speech.

上帝的沉默,让人的思想成熟为言语。

305

THOU wilt find, Eternal Traveller, marks of thy footsteps across my songs.

您将发觉,永恒的旅人,我的歌里注满了您的足音。

306

LET me not shame thee, Father, who displayest thy glory in thy children.

别让我使您蒙羞,天父,您在您的孩子身上显示了您的荣光。

307

CHEERLESS is the day, the light under frowning clouds is like a punished child with traces of tears on its pale cheeks, and the cry of the wind is like the cry of a wounded world. But I know I am travelling to meet my Friend.

郁郁寡欢的白天,眉头紧锁的云朵下的光,就像一个挨罚的孩子,苍白脸颊上留着泪痕;风的哭喊,就像受伤的世界在哭喊。而我知道,我正赶去会见我的教友。

308

TO-NIGHT there is a stir among the palm leaves, a swell in the sea, Full Moon, like the heart throb of the world. From what unknown sky hast thou carried in thy silence the aching secret of love?

今夜,棕榈的叶子一阵阵悸动,海涨了,月圆了,仿佛世界的心在搏动。从哪一片未知的天空,您用您的默默无言带来了教人隐隐作痛的爱的秘密?

309

I DREAM of a star, an island of light, where I shall be born and in the depth of its quickening leisure my life will ripen its works like the rice-field in the autumn sun.

我梦见一颗星辰,一座光之岛,我将在那里诞生,在它促发生机的安逸深处,我的人生将功德圆满,恰似秋阳下的稻田。

310

THE smell of the wet earth in the rain rises like a great chant of praise from the voiceless multitude of the insignificant.

雨中湿土的气味升起,仿佛微不足道的无言大千唱出的一首伟大赞歌。

311

THAT love can ever lose is a fact that we cannot accept as truth.

爱也会失去,这是一个我们无法当真接受的事实。

312

WE shall know some day that death can never rob us of that which our soul has gained, for her gains are one with herself.

我们终将明白,死神绝对夺不走我们灵魂所赢得的东西,因为她的所得已和她自身融为一体。

313

GOD comes to me in the dusk of my evening with the flowers from my past kept fresh in his basket.

在我黄昏的薄暮里,上帝来到我身边,带着在他篮子里依然鲜艳的我过往的花儿。

314

WHEN all the strings of my life will be tuned, my Master, then at every touch of thine will come out the music of love.

当我人生所有的琴弦一一调好之时,我的主,您的每一次触拨都将流出爱的乐音。

315

LET me live truly, my Lord, so that death to me become true.

让我真实地活着,我的主,好让死对我来说也成真实。

316

MAN'S history is waiting in patience for the triumph of the insulted man.

人类的历史,就是耐心等待受侮辱的人获胜。

317

I FEEL thy gaze upon my heart this moment like the sunny silence of the morning upon the lonely field whose harvest is over.

我感到此刻您注视着我的心,仿佛清晨明媚的寂静罩着那收获之后孤寂的田地。

318

I LONG for the Island of Songs across this heaving Sea of Shouts.

我渴望这呼啸的"呐喊之海"彼岸的"歌之岛"。

319

THE prelude of the night is commenced in the music of the sunset, in its solemn hymn to the ineffable dark.

夜的序曲,开启于夕阳的音乐,那献给不可直呼其名的黑暗的圣歌。

320

I HAVE scaled the peak and found no shelter in fame's bleak and barren height. Lead me, my Guide, before the light fades, into the valley of quiet where life's harvest mellows into golden wisdom.

我攀登过高峰,在声名荒秃的峰巅找不到庇护所。引领我,我的向导,在日光褪尽之前,进入安谧山谷,在那里人生的收获将纯熟成金色的智慧。

321

THINGS look phantastic in this dimness of the dusk—the spires whose bases are lost in the dark and tree tops like blots of ink. I shall wait for the morning and wake up to see thy city in the light.

万物在这薄暮冥冥中显得鬼影幢幢——底座消失在黑暗里的尖塔、仿佛墨渍的树梢。我将等到天明,醒来看您的城漾在光里。

322

I HAVE suffered and despaired and known death and I am glad that I am in this great world.

我受过难,绝望过,体会过死,我很高兴,生在这个伟大的人间。

323

THERE are tracts in my life that are bare and silent. They are the open spaces where my busy days had their light and air.

我的人生有一些光秃而寂静的地带。它们是我忙碌的日子里享受阳光和空气的空地。

324

RELEASE me from my unfulfilled past clinging to me from behind making death difficult.

把我从我未得圆满的过去解脱出来吧,它从背后死死缠着我,不让我痛快地死去。

325

LET this be my last word, that I trust in thy love.

就让这做我最后的话吧:我信赖您的爱。

译后记

松 风

要不是接受翻译任务，我与《飞鸟集》今生也许就这么错过了。上世纪60年代初我出生于长江北岸泊湖边一个贫穷的乡村，少年时代无缘见到任何真正意义上的文学名著，到了告别家乡外出求学的岁月，深感错过了读这类作品的年龄，私心里总以为《飞鸟集》是给孩子们读的。及至着手翻译之时，早已过了知天命的年纪，虽花甲既望，却没想到泰戈尔这些貌似清浅的诗句竟如此打动我。常常，译好一段，会不由自主地凝望窗外，神驰心远，仿佛进入了楼下小区院子里归鸟们的梦境。译泰戈尔，总让我忍不住冲动要对林间眠鸟们表白：莫不静好，与子同梦。

由此想到，一百多年前在整个孟加拉语世界享有盛誉的东方诗哲泰戈尔征服伦敦文学圈的情形。据2013年5月27日《双周评论》(*The Fortnight Review*)转载的威廉·罗森斯坦《泰戈尔在伦敦》一文叙述，罗森斯坦这位名重一时的英国评论家、艺术家偶然在《现代评论》上读到一篇署名泰戈尔的短篇小说，甚为喜爱，于是写信给杂志主编询问未来是否会刊登更多泰戈尔作品，很快收到一位中学校长翻译的泰戈尔诗稿笔记本。旅居伦敦的印度名流见此，力邀泰戈尔访英。泰戈尔将旅途中翻译的诗作送给罗森斯坦"笑纳"。泰戈尔简朴的修辞和凝重的哲思完全征服了罗森斯坦，罗森斯坦将这些诗稿出示给庞德、萧伯纳、布里奇斯等，并寄送大诗人叶芝，介绍他们相识。叶芝读了也极其喜爱，不吝溢美之词："谁要是说他可以完善这些作品，这人便不懂文学。"[1]据庞德发表在 1913 年 3 月《双周评论》上题为"拉宾德拉纳特·泰戈尔"一文披露，读到诗稿一个月后，庞德去叶芝住所，发现叶芝"为一个'比我们任何人都伟大'的伟大诗人的出现兴奋不已"。叶芝自己也在《吉檀迦利》英文版序里坦言："连日来我随身带着这些译稿，在火车上、公交车顶和餐馆里阅读，我不得不常常合上诗稿，生怕陌生人看出我是多么为之动容。这些抒情诗，其思想展示了一个我毕生梦寐以求的世界……一种传统，其间诗与宗教毫无分别。"

在罗森斯坦协调下，《吉檀迦利》英文版由伦敦印度学会出版，叶芝亲自审订泰戈尔译文，为之作序，更以其

---

[1] In Malcolm Sen: "Mythologising a 'mystic': W.B. Yeats on the poetry of Rabindranath Tagore", *History Ireland*, Issue 4, Volume 18, 2010.

强大影响力在伦敦文学圈广泛推介，使得该书一时"伦敦纸贵"，六个月内重印十次，掀起了一股泰戈尔热。等泰戈尔访美回到伦敦，发觉自己从一个寂寂无名的"英漂"变成了炙手可热的诗坛名流，被主流报纸呼作"诗圣"（poet and saint）。与此同时，旅居伦敦、身兼门罗主编的《诗刊》驻英记者的庞德，从第一现场频频向芝加哥发回"内幕消息"，不遗余力地向美国诗坛推介泰戈尔。

我深知，泰戈尔打动叶芝和西方读者的，肯定比打动我的那于清浅却飘忽的文字间流淌的诗情和哲思，更为深沉而宏博。也许是泰戈尔诗中弥漫着的宗教和奉献情怀，以及借由古老传统中感发出的现代敏感所揭示的超越民族和阶级分别的人类境况，神之手一般地拨动了困苦于现代化弊端中的叶芝们的心弦？正如泰戈尔生前好友，英国古典学权威吉尔伯特·默里在为《死亡之翼》英文版所作的序里所言，泰戈尔"是个真正的诗人，而且是个新型的诗人，他能使东方和西方的想象互相理解。他的天才是抒情的"。

关于如何理解泰戈尔及其《飞鸟集》，实力派青年学者戴潍娜女士做了深具历史感和学理的权威导读，我无须平添狗尾，只是忍不住要转引前辈译家吴岩先生《泰戈尔诗选》序言里援引的季羡林先生的评价：

尽管泰戈尔也受到西方哲学思潮的影响，但他的思想的基调，还是印度古代从《梨俱吠陀》一直到奥义书和吠檀多的类似泛神论的思想。这种思想主张宇宙万有，同源一体，这个一体就叫作"梵"。"梵"是宇宙万有的统一体，世界的本质。人与"梵"也是统一体。"'我'是'梵'的异名，'梵'是最高之'我'"。"人的实质同自然实质没有差别，两者都是世界本质'梵'的一个组成部分，互相依存，互相关联"。泰戈尔以神或"梵"为一方，称之为"无限"，以自然或现象世界以及个人的灵魂为一方，称之为"有限"，无限和有限之间的关系，是他哲学探索的中心问题，也是他诗歌中经常触及的问题。泰戈尔跟印度传统哲学不同的地方是：他把重点放在"人"上面，主张人固然需要神，神也需要人，甚至认为只有在人中才能见到神……既然梵我合一，我与非我合一，人与自然合一，其间的关系，也就是宇宙万有的关系，就只能是和谐与协调。和谐与协调可以说是泰戈尔思想的核心。

简单说一说翻译。作为一个不乏实践，自觉怀有敬畏之心的业余译者，我对翻译的悖论向来不敢稍忘。翻译的现实目的，无疑是消灭差异，但翻译的最高价值，恰恰在于保存差异。说翻译是文化间的桥梁,这桥不仅为彼此走进对方文化提供通途,更应促进彼此交融、相互生长。因此,在翻译过程中,我努力传达原作"说了什么",同时竭力体现原作"是如何说的"。我的追求是,不仅要以通达的汉语传译原作的内容,更试图传达原文的声音,它的腔调、它的气息和节奏,甚至它的模棱与含混。做过翻译的人都知道,这何其难哉。

先说说书名。Stray Birds,原意是"迷途的鸟",虽然迷途的鸟也是飞鸟,但飞鸟未必是迷途的鸟。而且,译作"飞鸟",多少遮蔽了原文也许隐藏着的呼唤与期盼,少了几分殷切。但"飞鸟集"这个译名已然经典化,撇开约定俗成不说,单就翻译技术而言也不好轻易挑战。不过,全书首句里我还是译作了"夏天迷途的鸟儿"。

《飞鸟集》英文原文,虽作者自译于《吉檀迦利》之后,理应较后者英文成熟,但不知泰戈尔有意无意,抑或孟加拉文语义过于丰繁(若是,倒可为英译中国古典诗词提供借鉴),不少句子的关键词甚至句子本身多义或者容易歧义,甚至有少数不合规范者。翻译中,不合规范者反而好办,难对付的是词或句的多义和歧义。做不到以多义译多义时,只好明晰化,或以一义译多义。比如:The dry river-bed finds no thanks for its past,至少应该包含两层意思,一是今天忘恩负义,一是过去乏善可陈,原译"干涸的河床,发觉它的过去无可感激",考虑到这样的汉语不容易为人接受,后改作"干涸的河床对它的过去毫无好感",而且取的是这个短语当代英语里已作废的义项。再如:Life is given to us, we earn it by giving it,原文 life 及其代词 it 被摆弄得颇有意味,我只能舍其味存其意译作"生命赐给了我们,我们付出生命赢得人生"。最让我纠结不定的,是"I have dipped the vessel of my heart into this silent hour; it has filled with love"一句。其中的 vessel of my heart,是"心舟",还是"心的容器",从语义和逻辑上看,两者皆可,因为 dipped 含有两层意思,一是"将……放低",一是"浸,蘸"。虽私心里更倾向"心舟",但最终还是选择了更安全的"心的容器"。还有一个颇费周折的句子,If you shed tears when you miss the sun, you also miss the stars,问题就在第一个 miss 有着双关意思(看不见,思念),但没有"错过"的意思,因为你一直在看着太阳落山,直至消失;第二个 miss 没有"思念"的意思,但"错过"的含义强于"看不见",而且前后之间用了个 also 修饰。综合考虑只好译作"倘若看不见太阳时你落泪,你也看不见星星"。一首智利民歌歌词可以做这一句的注释:当太阳消失时别哭泣,你的泪水会让你看不见星星。

泰戈尔还使用或创造了有一些在英文原文里很传神的表达，我试着依此拓展汉语表达。如"Not hammerstrokes, but dance of the water sings the pebbles into perfection"译作"将卵石唱得珠圆玉润的，是水的舞曲，而非丁丁锤声"。第301节里的Thy sunshine smiles upon the winter days of my heart，同理，径译作"您的阳光将微笑洒到我心的冬日"。再如第168节等，译文的表达方式亦依循原文，意在丰富汉语表达。

此前虽未通读过《飞鸟集》，如此流行的经典自然难免耳濡目染，比如"生如夏花般绚烂，死如秋叶般静美"早已深入人心，翻译中没有勇气刻意回避，倒是直接采用。在此，对前辈的贡献深表敬意和谢意。

感谢中国社会科学院外国文学研究所时任所长陈众议先生所率领的主编团队邀请我重译《飞鸟集》，同时感谢苏玲编审邀请青年学者、诗人戴潍娜女士拨冗"导读"，戴潍娜女士的导读为拙译增色多多，深表感谢。感谢王竞女士费心统筹，感谢责任编辑赵庆丰先生严谨细致的编审，他的认真和专业避免了拙译的可能差错，还感谢他以专业眼光挑选的插图。

最后，祝读者朋友阅读愉快。泰戈尔也许是读者最友好型的经典作家，无论何时展卷，他的文字都会给你或心有灵犀或幡然醒悟式的惊喜。泰戈尔会启迪你：当万千迷狂，你的目光当注视那安静的；当众足齐踩，你的心当牵系那悄然离去的；当两相对决，你的天平当不欺侮那势弱的。